The Lucky Thirteen

AJ Vosse

ISBN: 9781521982655
Imprint: Independently published by AJ Vosse

Table of Content

For you – the Special One and Editor in Chief!

An Ordinary Man

James J stared at the deluge lashing the windowpanes. The longer he stared the louder the noise became. The glass seemed to vibrate, adding to his sense of impending doom. He wondered if the rain and hail would crack a pane. He suspected that once the elements breached the flimsy defences they would then tear into the room. No, he thought, not if, rather when.

The white missiles clattered relentlessly into the vertical obstruction man had placed in its path. Would his shelter withstand the onslaught? Would the wind keep increasing in intensity, thus aiding the missiles as they drove into his protection?

"Bloody hell, bloody almighty damnation!"

He roared at the din. No, his futile attempts didn't even make a dent in the decibel level. He knew his attempt at retaliation was foolish and wasted yet it gave him momentary relief. Of what he wasn't too sure but at that moment in time he thought he felt better.

"I screamed at you, you foul thing hurling your abuse at me. I screamed at you!"

He slumped back into the old leather recliner he'd earlier positioned near the window so he could watch the fury.

"Bloody hell..."

This time his tone was hushed, muted by the howling all around. The little cottage seemed to quake at the onslaught directly off the icy Atlantic. What a place to seek solitude! No radios, no phones, no music. No way of communicating with civilisation. Boy, did he get his hideout just right. Imagine Mother Nature flattening the place. No one would know he'd been swept into the sea.

He pulled the old grey army blanket closer around him. Everything was old in this place. He tried to make himself a little more comfortable without using his hands. Each time he thought he'd found the best spot on the lumpy padding another broken spring seemed to find a tender spot on his posterior.

"Bloody storm, bloody cottage... bloody recliner! Bloody everything..."

Another momentary tension release as he howled at the storm.

"Bloody fool!"

Yes, he thought, he was the bloody fool to be sitting here on this desolate island.

So much for the navy suggesting that he hide out here for a few weeks. Easy for them, sneak in with a sub, drop him off with enough supplies and do a runner to their warm beds. Why did he ever get involved? For what exactly?

They'd cover his back, they said.

The whole escapade took 18 months to put together. Now, here he was sitting, staring at the missiles that must surely break down his flimsy defences and kill him in the process. All because his life had become so boring that he'd started messing on the internet. One evening he'd got so fed up with the cheap, low grade porn he was watching that he decided he'd try a few new tricks.

"Assassin for hire"

The simple three-word phrase in the search bar was enough the get the ball rolling. A snowball which in turn triggered a rock fall that upset the mountainside, resulting in an avalanche of devastating proportion.

James stared at the glass panes while the storm outside turned into one of those weather phenomena the clever folk call 200 hundred year events. Some event, his death was going to be. The frothy, foamy sea out there must have his number. Well, that was debatable he thought, more likely the wind and hail will get him first. He could vaguely make out the crashing waves only 30 meters away. The curtain of driving hail partially masked the foam and sea spray.

An alarm bell rang somewhere in the dark recesses of his scrambled mind.

"Move... get into the coal pit, while you still have an opportunity!"

Yet he sat… mesmerised by the storm, bewitched by the idea of watching his own death scene unfolding.

***

"Harry... HARRY! Get over here, will you?"

Oliver screeched his request. His excitement causing an outbreak of emotion totally unlike his normal behaviour. He watched Harry hurriedly making his way between the trench excavation and rubble spoil heaps.

"What's got you so excited Ollie?"

"I think I've found the answer, that's what's got me so excited."

He revealed the small leather-bound notebook he'd been holding behind his back.

"This notebook is remarkably preserved, considering it's been in this pit for more than a hundred and fifty years. I have a feeling the large stone slabs must have prevented moisture getting at it for all these years."

"Where did you find it?"

"Concealed in the inner breast pocket of the old duffle coat"

The two men stood looking down at the skeletal remains. The woollen coat must surely have helped with the preservation of the notebook. Harry noticed something else. It seemed as if a glass shard had been dislodged when Olly opened up the coat.

"Look at that."

"Yes, it seems to me the glass shards actually stapled the coat shut when they lodged in our friend's torso."

"So, you think the answer to the mystery will be in that little book?"

Ollie glanced at Harry. It seemed as if the expectancy may even have turned into happy acceptance. It would be great if the team leader could eventually find a positive to report back on.

"Well, we've found very few clues to date. You'll have to agree; this is one of those excavations that seemed to be going nowhere."

Harry nodded in agreement. Ollie wondered if he noticed signs of relief in Harry's eyes.

"Yep, I'm with you on that one. There have been mighty few clues to cast any light on what seemed to be another unsolved mystery for the team. Let's hope we can find an answer or two so we can wind up the dig."

The two stood, again looking down at the mystery skeleton. Who was he? Why was he on the island in the North Atlantic and how on earth did he die. Well, that answer seemed to be staring them in the face.

"Let's cover our friend up again and find shelter in the galley tent."

Ollie did as Harry suggested before following his team lead to the tent. He could do with a coffee anyhow so the idea of meeting in the tent was a good one. He found Harry at the table closest to the light, the man seemingly already engrossed in the contents of the notebook.

"Sit."

He gestured absentmindedly as Ollie pulled up a chair, wondering if he was supposed to remain standing.

"Sorry, you must think me rude, of course you must sit."

Harry passed the notepad over,

"Look there, seems you're right. This may well be the find of the century. I think our man has let us into a secret that could redefine our take on the happenings that shaped history all those years ago."

Ollie read the passage Harry pointed out.

"Wow! If this is true its incendiary stuff. Thank goodness we're only finding it now. Could you imagine the ramifications of our friend's actions if they were discovered soon after the event?"

The two men sat, sipping silently at their coffee, while reflecting on the information before them. They both realised this news would go global as it answered a question left in the dark for more than 150 years. Harry broke the silence after what seemed hours.

"OK, we have much to do. I think we'll put in a few more days tidying up the excavation and at the same time I'll arrange for the museum director to organise a news conference here on the island in about ten days' time."

Harry paused a few seconds to observe Ollie's reaction before continuing.

"You happy with that? That should give you enough time to complete the research and the dig."

Ollie nodded, not daring to open his mouth for fear of blurting out something stupid. His emotions churned. Imagine… him in front of the world's press. Imagine his 3D images being beamed to all parts of the world. He was on the verge of becoming a star. He'd found the notepad so he could decide the fate of the discovery. He could place the find on the open market. He'd be rich! Rich and famous. Not bad, he thought, for a junior archaeologist in his late twenties, not bad at all.

Harry's gentle nudge and knowing wink brought him back to reality.

"Yes, the rewards could be substantial but there's still a bit to be done."

***

Ollie watched the press group making their way from the dig site into the meeting room that had been set up for their press release. Fortunately, it was a warm dry day so the sides of the temporary structure were open, allowing a faint breeze to cool down the space. He was going to need all the cooling he could get, he mused. Soon he'd have to face that group of inquisitive individuals who would all want to ask *the* scoop question.

He watched Harry and the museum director at the rear of the group. The two men were in animated discussion. He could only imagine what was being said. He expected they'd be hoping for a cut of the financial gains he'd stand to make once the world knows about the contents of the notepad.

Harry made his way to the front of the meeting area and waved his arms to silence the gathering folk.

"Please folk, would you take your seats as soon as possible?"

He waited a few moments until the hush died down.

"I'd like to introduce Professor Hugh Mc Morris, the Director of

Operations at London's Euro Museum of History. Hugh will fill in the background information before Ollie reveals the details of the finds. Please feel free to ask questions at any time. Just raise a hand and we'll answer as we go along."

Hugh waited for the brief applause to end before beginning.

"Greetings all. Where do we begin? I think, before we get to the fellow in the shelter out there, let me fill you in with the reason for doing an actual dig and not the normal, nonintrusive, virtual fact-finding mission."

Hugh turned, paused and pointed in Ollie's direction.

"Ollie had a hunch right from word go that we'd uncover factual evidence that could only be recovered by digging. His hunch turned out to be about 150% correct. OK, back to why we have you here."

"You've all seen the skeletal remains out there in the dig. Let's begin with how our friend came to meet his end. We've looked back at historical weather records and pinpointed the storm that most likely resulted in the collapse of the cottage".

Hugh turned toward Harry and gestured at the raised stage. Within seconds the holographic 3D figure of a man seated in a recliner appeared. The static crackle in the room soon settled into a barely audible hum as the image projectors warmed to their synchronised task.

"Harry, would you please turn Mr X to face outward... OK, now add the rest of the missing pieces."

Hugh watched the 3D imagery taking shape before turning back to face his captive audience.

"Right... now we have Mr X seated as he was, staring out at the storm lashing the cottage. The metrological details we've unearthed confirm that the forces on the cottage were so severe that an implosion resulted."

Hugh paused to look around the room. Yes, they all seemed enthralled so he gestured to the image on the stage.

"OK... we'll begin the animation now..."

The roaring of the storm erupted. Hail clattered into the 3D's simulated window. Within seconds the first pane shattered. This set off a chain reaction. The remaining panes disintegrated almost simultaneously. The wind drove the glass shards into Mr X, killing him instantly. He stood no chance. He absorbed the full fury of the storm damage.

Quiet returned at Hugh's signal.

"We've looked at the storm data while producing the simulation. What you have just witnessed must have been as close to true speed as the actual event. Mr X would've seen the first pane give way but we

doubt he as much as blinked before being riddled by shards."

Hugh stopped. He'd noticed one of the press members at the rear raising his arm.

"Seems you have a question..."

"Indeed. It's all good and well you telling us all of this but really, what relevance has the death of one man on a remote island have on dragging us here?"

"Aha, impatient for answers, are you?"

A few more murmurs confirmed the press contingent's growing restlessness.

"OK, we brought you all here to see where we unearthed one of the most important pieces of information relating to events just before the storm destroyed the cottage. We're convinced the storm devastating the island took place in late mid-June 2016.

Silence descended, Hugh waited to see if any of the press group would piece together what those events were.

"Who's the fellow out there in the excavation? He seems to be the link to something... but how?"

Hugh took a step closer to the group in an attempt to identify the questioner.

"Let me put it this way, he was just an ordinary man. An ordinary man who'd got himself involved in the events. James J Wilson, a Londoner who'd somehow managed to get dragged into the chapters of 21st century history, even though his identity is only now coming to light."

"At this point I'm handing proceedings to Oliver Begley. As you know by now, Ollie was the one who discovered the information. Ollie, they're all yours."

Ollie cleared this throat, took a last sip of water before beginning.

"Hello all. I'd like to begin by reading an extract from a notepad found concealed in the coat our friend James was wearing at the time of his death. Before we get to that, just a brief mention of why we chose to dig here on this isolated island. I'm a naval archaeologist and stumbled upon the logbooks of the sub that dropped James here. The dates and one mention of a man dropped on this island set the ball rolling."

Ollie cleared his throat again, trying his utmost to hide his heightened state of nervousness. He removed the notepad from its protective sheath and opened it where he'd placed a bookmark.

> "The navy rescuers were true to their word. The extraction plan was actioned as soon as the shots found their target. The confusion caused by the shots and the diversion created by the

ground operatives allowed just enough time for my escape. Within minutes of leaving the 3rd floor room I was led to a waiting police car. The car simply switched on its sirens and lights and drove away from the scene."

"Within thirty minutes I was ushered into a waiting helicopter. The uneventful flight ended somewhere along the coast where a dinghy was waiting to take me to the sub. I slept most of the time on the sub so I don't really have a clue how long it took before I was dropped on the island. The navy had seen to everything."

Ollie was about to continue when another pressman interrupted.

"Would I be right in saying that May 2016 was the beginning of what later generations referred to as Armageddon?"

The room erupted into a cacophony of startled voices. Simultaneous questions were directed at Ollie and the rest of the archaeology team. It took a few minutes before calm descended.

"OK all, if we can get you to address your question in a controlled fashion we will endeavour to answer. Yes, in our estimation Mr James J Wilson was the catalyst. He was the instrument that set off what some historians refer to as World War Three."

"How can you be so sure?"

"All the evidence is recorded in the notepad. James J documented it all once he arrived on the island. He makes reference to smuggling the notebook in the hem of his overcoat. He definitely wanted his story to be found."

"You've referred to the navy on a few occasions. Am I correct in assuming it to be the Brits?"

"Yes, all the information points at that. Notes of conversations he'd had with the special forces indicate that the Brits felt they needed to do the dirty in such a way that blame would be pointed at other forces and in so doing they would get a reaction to suit their needs."

At this point Hugh interrupted.

"We know from history that the threat of IS was spreading rapidly. Coupled with this, the unrest in the Ukraine seemed to be linked with IS. History suggests Putin allowed IS to infiltrate and destabilise the region. The Brits and French were worried that all their interests in the Middle East were simply evaporating, consumed by the mess in Syria and Turkey. If you can recall, most of the countries surrounding the Black Sea were at that stage dragged into the wholescale terror onslaught."

Hugh let his words sink in for a few moments.

"It's against this backdrop that our story unfolds."

He paused, stepping back to allow Ollie to answer the questions, as yet another question was asked.

"What did the Brits stand to gain?"

"Seemingly, they wanted Russia and the United States to drop their feud about Syria and the Ukraine and stand together with Europe in fighting the fundamentalist terror tide that was threatening to engulf the Middle East and spread to Eastern Europe and North Africa."

"How can you be so sure the Brits arranged the whole thing? Surely we must believe what history suggests. Surely it was the forces unleashed by fundamentalist terrorism that sparked the outbreak of the all-out war in the Middle East?"

Ollie remained silent, taking note of the confused looks on some of the faces. Seems some were recalling what they knew about the key event that set off Armageddon.

"Let me give you a quick summary of events before I read the final passage from the notebook. The Brits got together with the French and Germans to invite the Russian and American Presidents to talk to each other. Apparently, it took the three main European powers more than a year to set up the meeting."

"After much debate and planning they actually got agreement. The Brits had planted the seeds. Why not meet in France? Why not meet in Reims? Why not in early May? The German Chancellor kicked up a fuss at first but the Brits and French convinced her. They pointed out that a meeting in the place where the German WW Two surrender was signed would show solidarity. It would show that all was forgiven and that united Britain, France and Germany, together with the US and Russia, could tackle the new threat they faced."

Ollie paused again. He looked around at the press group. Here and there he thought he saw knowing looks. Could a few be working out where he was heading?

"Of course, all this allowed the British Secret Service time to set up the plot. They trained James. They placed sniper's rifles in preselected locations in the town. This allowed them different options to choose from closer to the date."

One of the pressmen at the rear of the group could no longer contain his curiosity.

"How do you know all of this?"

Ollie lifted the notebook for all to see.

"Our friend James recorded all the happenings. Seems he paid close attention to all that was said and done. As I mentioned before, it appears as if he wanted the truth to be out at some point. Seems the

Brits hoped that his actions would spark the retaliation they wanted."

An uneasy silence descended once more. Ollie allowed the gathering a minute or so to reflect on all that had been revealed.

"I'll not bore you with anymore of the details of the planning but I'll briefly remind you of the hit. The site chosen for the signing of the cooperation accord was the Reims Town Hall. The Brits knew there was a large open town square in front of the Mairie de Reims."

"This allowed them to install James in a room on the top floor of the building, on the corner of Rue de Pouilly and Rue Dr Jacquin, as the streets were then named. The sighting angle was perfect for when the five leaders made their public appearances."

Ollie paused, noticing that the silence seemed to intensify. The gathering was waiting in a state of suspended silence. Their facial expressions told him they would most likely be ready for the tale's climax. He stretched the silence for effect.

"OK, I'll read the final entry in the notepad and then we can have a question session if that suits your needs."

Ollie paused again, maximising the drama of the moment. He opened the notebook, took a step back as if bracing himself for the reaction he expected. He looked at the gathered press contingent one more time before he began reading.

> "I wonder if my story will ever be believed, that it was me, James Jeramiah Wilson, an ordinary man who did the deed. Would people believe that I pulled the trigger, not once but twice, in rapid succession? Pulled the trigger that killed both the presidents… Obama and Putin, together they died for the Queen's cause."

Do Nothing

"Sergeant, what exactly is that soldier doing?"

"Nothing, Sir..."

He'd expected the startled expression. Here in the military, men aren't supposed to do nothing, so when an officer sees nothing being done it spells trouble. The sergeant purposely allowed the prolonged pause to drag on. He allowed the tension to mount until it became almost tangible. He allowed the oppressively hot, humid heavy air to add to the drama of the moment, as if the smoke of 20 cannons expelling their toxic vapour suffocated any thoughts of reality.

Sergeant Ross glanced at the rosy cheeked man standing beside him. He'd deliberately planned for the familiarisation walk to end here in the shade of a tree about 15 meters from where the young soldier was sitting. The soldier was dressed only in a pair of shorts and a stained, sun parched shirt. Nondescript, barely visible against the background of the surrounding thicket of woodland, part of the land, rather than just visiting.

The sergeant's thoughts turned again to the new arrival. The uniform crisp, only months old, unlike his faded combat dress that although neat, was well past their best days. Damn, why can't they stop sending him these kids? Soldiering is not for babies, especially now as the conflict was intensifying on all fronts.

They seem to make them younger each year, he mused. He reflected briefly on the seemingly insane process of sending children fresh out of secondary school on officer's course. Conscription was so cruel. Perform well at your good school and you'd most likely end up in some officer's college somewhere back home before your molars were out of their sockets. Then, next stop? War. In a faraway, forsaken edge of the continent, light-years away from the comforts of home and mommy's cooking and care.

"Damn!"

He again muttered under his breath. How many more years will he have to lead these kids into battle, just how many more years will it take for the warlords to continue demanding more death from their nation? How many more years will the politicians throw the youth of the country at the enemy's guns?

He cut short his mental ramblings to glance over at Lieutenant Pendleton. His gaze was again drawn to the mere smudge of a moustache. So young! Only a fresh faced boy yet now he was supposed to understand what he was seeing. How the blazes can any man understand what they were witnessing? How much more, thought

Sergeant Ross, just how much more difficult must it be for a fellow to see the horrid results of conflict when he has never set his foot outside the safe zone?

"We've left him to his own devices while we wait for the Medics to make up their minds. He lives out here beneath the trees."

Sergeant Ross gestured at the lush green world at the edge of the base camp. Here, many miles away from the dangers of the frontline, it was easy to close one's eyes and imagine oneself enjoying the luxuries of a subtropical safari camp.

He turned his head slowly, until he fixed his eyes on the shell of the man-boy seemingly relaxing in the shade of a massive old tree. Just months ago, *that* young man was also an eager, fresh-faced soldier arriving at the front, ready for his own conquest of destiny. Now he was a silent shadow of those aspirations.

"Sir... the lad's not responding to any human interaction. He shuns all contact, yet... there he is, existing only meters away from his peers."

Again, the sergeant let the heat laden billows of silence waft into the mental spaces, seeping into every dark crevice of their minds. His was battle weary; the young lieutenant's dazed and disorientated by his first brushes with the reality that was war.

The pause dragged wearily on. Eventually Sergeant Ross turned slightly, to get a better look at the young man standing beside him. The rosiness was gone. In its place an ashen likeness of what minutes before was the innocent, fresh brightness of an eager young officer.

Maybe this one will learn quickly, thought Sergeant Ross. Maybe he'll learn and realise there is no glory in war; there are no hero's, dead or alive. Maybe he'll learn that Hemingway's words were true, no matter how just war was, it was ultimately still crime. Maybe the lieutenant will grasp that no matter how much one's debt and loyalty to the flag one swears allegiance to is elevated in college one's own kin still bleed and die the same way as the enemy.

After years of combat the sergeant was used to seeing blood, to seeing the remains of his troops scattered on the red earth... and in the trees. He'd watched men lance the enemy with blunt bayonets. He's seen hate, love... longing... lust for life... depravity. Is that not the lack of love? Depravity? He's seen almost all there is to see.

Or, had he? Had he yet another new frontier to see? The intangible barrier, the divide between the rational and the dim, dingy dark distance of derange.

"Is he reacting to anything... anything in the slightest?"

"No Sir. No... the lad seems oblivious. Totally withdrawn from this life. Like a tortoise that's pulled its head back into its shell, still alive but not functioning. He's there... he eats what's put out for him. He knows to drink... no beer, no soft drinks, only water. He's even in control of his hygiene... sneaks into the ablutions in the middle of the night. He's become totally primeval... yet, he somehow knows how to stick to the basics."

The young lieutenant turned toward Sergeant Ross. His imploring eyes demanding a better explanation. He held the sergeant's gaze as best he could even as the bitter bile of revulsion crept its way into his parched mouth.

"Sergeant, I see the shell of a man who's most likely not many months older than me. I see dead eyes, I sense an aura of death all around, well, I think that's what I sense, please help me here. They speak of death at the college but how is a man supposed to ever be ready for seeing something like this? How, when the man has only stepped off the transporter only hours before?"

Lieutenant Pendleton gasped, as if the turgid, stale air enveloping them had forced its way into his lungs and was choking him.

Just how could he be ready? No, thought Sergeant Ross, no books or words could ever school anyone in the effects of war's death and destruction. Never.

This time it was the young lieutenant who let the pause linger. Sergeant Ross didn't break the silence. He respected the young officer's attempts at coming to terms with what he was experiencing.

"Sergeant, we're standing here talking about a person. Yes, I'm having my difficulties dealing with the situation but he is after all still a human, is he not?"

He glanced at Sergeant Ross for reassurance. Yes, the nod was slow but strong, affirming the greying soldier's agreement.

"Why has he chosen this spot to live? Is there any likely reason or did it just happen?"

"We're not really sure Sir. Tom was first kept in the sickbay after returning from the front."

Sergeant Ross turned and pointed at the neat white buildings at the edge of the woodland. He swung his arm from the direction of the buildings to the woodland,

"The lad soon began climbing out the windows at night to wander around in this thicket. As if he was searching for his soul or maybe as if he was searching for his brother. Who knows?"

He paused again, just long enough to catch his breath.

"See that shirt. The stains? He wouldn't allow medics to take the shirt. He would scream and perform so much that he'd upset the others around so he still wears it. The stains, as you may have guessed, are his brother's blood stains."

Sergeant Ross fell silent; he'd no more to add to the sad story.

"Sergeant, what's the man's name?"

"Tom, Infantryman Thomas James Barker. His brother was Infantryman Jeremy William Barker. Yes, they were as inseparable as the cartoon characters, until Jerry stepped on the landmine."

"Tom?" The lieutenant's lingering pause turned to a semi plea... *"Tom?"*

"Don't bother Sir, just don't. Tom's spirit was blown totally out of his core during that ambush. Only the physical form returned. Tom... he's long gone. Gone with his twin brother who was blown into a million bits. I saw it happen... the lad walked out of the ambush... covered with the remains of his brother. Tom walked out, blood-stained, as if in a mist of red death... "

"What shall we do for him?"

"Nothing Sir... we do nothing... for now."

Sergeant Ross stood... ramrod, rigid, straight. He stood, wondering when he'd ever walk out from beneath the cloud of his own brother's death. A death too long ago to remember, yet raw in his mind. His own brother, his baby brother, shot by a sniper as they entered the safety of their forward command post.

"Nothing Sir. For Tom you do nothing. No, all you need do is send two letters home... let the parents mourn all at once. One shock for them is more than enough... "

Lieutenant Templeton whispered as he turned to walk away,

"Nothing Tom, for you we'll do nothing."

The Severance Package

John B Smith stared at the grey partitioning of his office. His cell, as he so lovingly referred to the four meter squared space. His prison away from the other prison he called home. He followed one of the raised vertical threads of the fabric covering the partitioning wall. To think, this office décor had once been high corporate fashion. To think that he'd moved into this space at about the same time as the shopfitters completed the installation.

Twenty three years had taken their toll on the fabric. Twenty three long years had passed of this never-ending life sentence imposed on his miserable life. Bitter-bile recrimination flowed through his head like torrents of molten lava… searing the last bits of joy from his muddled mind.

The grey line in the raised fabric merged into vague infinity at the top of the divide. He could hear the muffled movement of the neighbouring cubicle's occupant. Layla Mae, how sweet a name for such a gross human being. Gross, short, rotund, vodka soaked peroxide blond. Foulmouthed and uncouth, loud, low-class unrefined bitch. A common slapper, flotsam cast aside after the last liberation wave washed over the sordid council estate where she was spawned.

"Slut… fucking street-whoring, syphilitic slut!"

"Shut your fucking mouth you dumb-arsed useless waste of a pale skin knob-head… just shut the fuck up!"

John sat bolt upright. His bewildered emotions churned into a frenzy by the cesspool of vitriol brewing in his soul. He realised he must've expressed his angst rather than confining his thoughts to where they best belonged.

He listened as the noises grew louder. The laptop slammed shut; almost simultaneously he heard it being wrenched from its docking station.

"Let me take myself outta this crap pit before I slap the useless fucker back into his mother's dirty hole. Stupid, worthless prick! Be sure you'll hear a word or two from HR, you ignorant cretin."

***

Two days later the summons arrived. The meeting, in Block B Room 2-214, scheduled for 14h30 on Friday the 24th, would set in motion a chain of events such had never been seen in any small coastal town in Ireland. Life changing events, all because of his six word outburst.

John knew he was bound to get more than he deserved because of his misendeavour. The company's ever tightening political correctness policies were no longer a joke. The whole HR trip at the place had become stiflingly restrictive. One could expect a written warning for a slightly below the belt jibe so his six word tirade was likely to receive the pinnacle of company censure.

Oh well, change was well overdue but how was he to face the consequences? How was he, John B Smith, to break out of the mould? How was he to overcome almost 35 years of fears and phobias and move? How does a man who has never set foot inside a motorised vehicle, of any kind, change the fears of a lifetime?

The evening before the meeting he walked home. Slowly. He passed by the corner store and stopped in for the obligatory bread and milk. Another habit of a lifetime. Ever since he'd witnessed the death of his father, two blocks away from the store, he'd walked home this particular way. He'd *never* set foot near *that* horrid place *ever* again.

That was 35 years ago, to the month. The horrific killing of the only man he'd ever loved. The drunk driver had hurtled around the corner far too quickly. In the precious seconds before impact, his brave father had managed to lift John and fling him away with all his might. John came around seconds later to see the severed head of his father rolling slowly toward him.

That's how his mother found him. The heartbroken little boy, clutching the bloody head of his father to his heaving chest.

That evening John sat in the kitchen of the house where he'd lived his entire life. Change was knocking at the door; of that he was acutely aware. *That* six letter expletive string seemed to have galvanised all his energies into admitting that if he ever wanted to find some comfort from the lifelong pain then he'd have to break a few mental shackles. Quickly!

***

Three months paid leave of absence with immediate effect. The verdict seemed rather mild at first but as Sarah Moran, the HR person, stated at the meeting,

"We've taken a few things into account. Your behaviour up to this point has been exemplary. You also happen to be a minority shareholder. Almost 25 years is a long time so the board has decided to suggest that you take a break while a final solution is sought."

That was that. He returned to his cube to lock away the few effects he wasn't going to bother taking along with him. He walked to the coffee dock to rinse his mug. While there he noticed the oversized beaker used as a teacup by her ladyship, the foulmouthed Layla Mae. A sudden urge took hold of him, an urge to shove the mug up one of her orifices. The one that caused the most pain would be the best preferred!

Oh well, it was Friday so he would act as if the weekend had started a few hours earlier than normal. To celebrate, he'd walked the long way home and collected a few cans of brew and a naggin of hooch at the offie. He reasoned that as change was about to take a hold of his life he may as well shake a few things up on his own. Like beginning the weekend with a few brews.

Forty-five minutes after the meeting ended he was sitting at the kitchen table in the little house he called home. Three months! *Three months?* What was he to do during that time? He'd never taken more than ten day's holiday at any time in his life. Even in his secondary school days he'd worked during the breaks. What now?

John cracked open a can before reaching for the remote. He switched the TV on and flicked through the channels until he found the history programs. Now, there was the future, he thought to himself. Travel writing about historic sights.

"But John B Smith, you can't bear the thought of travel, apart from walking, so how could you ever become a travel writer?"

He didn't mind having this one-sided conversation with himself. In fact, as he had grown up he'd developed the habit as a way of interacting with his thoughts. He'd never had friends, never seen the need to complicate his life with the troubles of others. Many years ago, he'd overheard his mother explain the reason to one of the many men who'd passed through the front door.

"We think it is the emotional trauma of the accident that has permanently scarred Johnny."

Till this day he wonders who the *"we"* were.

"We think nothing! Who *ever* bothered to ask *me* how *I* felt?"

There was no counselling, no therapy sessions. Within weeks of the ordeal he'd asked his mother to allow him to return to school. The whole town knew about the accident so fortunately everyone left him alone. No one asked questions and he soon realised that as long as he kept to himself the others would keep their distance.

"OK Johnny B, what will you do with yourself for the next three months? Why not make a list of all the activities you've been longing to get involved with?"

His own sarcasm didn't go unnoticed on himself.

"Listen to yourself, after two tinnies your character has changed to nasty! Mind you, if this new Friday experiment's outcome is exponential, I'll be a raging lunatic when all this grog is done this evening!"

He sat for a few minutes, staring distractedly at the TV. Some

WW1 program about the toxins used during the Battle of the Somme.

"Now there will be a good place to visit and write about. Soon all the centenary celebrations will be taking place. Mind you, if I want to get there I'd have to slow down on this grogging and get something to eat. Chipper? Pizza? No, why not be brave and take a stroll to the pub to grab a bite?"

The seed for the events to come was planted while John sat waiting for his steak, egg and chips to arrive. He absentmindedly picked up a copy of the previous weekend's "Indo." By the time his food arrived he'd discarded the paper but not before sending himself a text containing just one five letter word.

Ricin

***

Within 30 seconds of waking on the Saturday morning John was fully back to his senses. He felt a tad groggy but quickly recalled the previous evening's fun.

"Now John boyo, not in many a year had you yourself such a pleasant evening. The food was great, the music good and you even had to fight off the advances of a half sozzled thirty something lass. Some evening!"

He shook his head slowly from side to side, smiling at his own strength of character. As usual he'd kept well to himself but when the music spun its charm and the feet began tapping he couldn't help but relax a little. That's when the attractive lady grabbed him by the arm for an impromptu dance.

He'd soon realised he had a choice or two to make. Allow her to entice him from behind his reserve walls and see where he would end up or flee rapidly back into his solitude. He quickly let the lady know how uncomfortable it was for some gays to make physical contact with women. His little ruse worked a charm. Within minutes he'd been allowed to return to his anonymity. Seemingly, the lady had whispered her hot news to a few bystanders who in turn spread the latest gossip. He'd enjoyed the rest of the evening in the relative peace of his own company. Sometime before closing time he's slipped out unnoticed and walked home.

His thoughts returned to the present. He had much to do. It didn't take him long to refresh himself in the shower before returning to his favourite room in the house. He made himself a few slices of toast as well as a mug of strong black coffee, then settled at the kitchen table again. He welcomed the background noise of the TV which he hadn't even bothered to switch off the previous evening.

He flicked through the channels but quickly decided to go for music. As soon as he'd selected one of the classic rock channels he reached for his laptop. He opened up the search engine and typed one word into the search bar.

Ricin

He was soon totally engrossed in what he found. The highly toxic poison could be made in a domestic kitchen by someone with a basic understanding of chemistry. All the ingredients and tools were freely available. So much so that at least on two separate occasions people sent envelopes containing the stuff to President Obama and a few others in the States.

He was fascinated by all the tales and myths he uncovered. The longer he read the more he wanted to read. He even found simple instruction from the American Patent Office. Yes, the information was all there. Easy to find and seemingly easy to manufacture one of the deadliest toxins on the planet.

By mid-afternoon information overload set in. He grabbed his hat and windbreaker and went out for a walk. He chose the path down to the wooded beach walk. High summer in Ireland was so good, once it wasn't raining. He'd walked less than one mile before finding what he was looking for. Against the south facing, high perimeter walls of the golf club grew the plants that supplied the main raw ingredient for ricin. The Castor Oil plant. That was how simple it was, he decided. He had all the answers but he needed to begin working on his major stumbling block. His aversion for all things mechanical transport!

He walked on and soon realised he was humming. He couldn't remember the words but found himself mouthing the opening line over and over,

"Ladies and gentlemen, this is Captain Tobias Wilcock"

He stopped dead in his tracks. Had he been humming something about going to Barbados? Or maybe even Bermuda?

John B Smith. The only thing that distinguished him from the countless John Smiths of this world was that "B". B for Bermuda! His mother had for years regaled all who wanted to listen with the tale of how he came to be blessed with a second name of Bermuda. A short story really,

"We honeymooned there. John was conceived on the island during a wild stormy night so that's how we came to name the little fellow John Bermuda. Cute, don't you think?"

"Cute, my hole!" John snarled softly.

He walked on for a few hours. His mind so full of ideas and plans that he felt he could walk all day. He realised he'd not felt so alive in a very long time. If ever, really. What seemed to give him an extra kick was the idea that within 24 hours of effectively being sacked and not knowing how he was going to cope with the time off he'd began a plan of revenge so surprising that he was excited by the prospects and the outcome of the future events.

"Bermuda John, bringer of justice!"

***

John spent the best part of the first week of his enforced leave of absence researching all the angles. Ricin may well be a deadly toxin but it soon lost viability so how was he going to get it administered and still have enough time to make his departure without capture or detection?

Ricin, the magic potion. Ricin, the answer to his problems. Ricin, the stuff of legend and urban myth.

He first thought of getting it into the teabags and coffee containers which were stocked in the tea stations at work but discarded this idea after quite a few references suggested the toxin was neutralised by temperatures above 80ºC.

Not only would he have to find a way to get the fresh toxin distributed in the office area but he'd have to find the most effective route into their bodies.

"This is going to be tricky, very tricky! Timing and method are going to be critical."

He often muttered while he was trawling through all the information. At one point he fleetingly wondered if the neighbours ever heard his chatter. He turned the TV volume up, just in case.

The major problem would be getting to the main targets without affecting too many of the other workers. Layla Mae needed special consideration. Then he'd also have to consider top management and those infernal HR people who only seemed to worry about how to make the lives of others difficult with all their politically correct claptrap.

"Bastards all… all must feel the wrath of justice."

***

John took frequent walks along the coastal paths to keep track of the seed formation of the castor oil plants he'd identified for harvesting. There were quite a few large plants that could be approached from well clear of the path and so doing allow him to go about his work unseen. He preferred harvesting the seeds rather than ordering ingredients via the internet.

All his planning revolved around doing things to prevent any form of trail being left. He was going to pull off the perfect revenge and get away with it, of that he was more and more certain. Planning was critical. Every detail needed research; every plan needed a backup or alternative approach.

It took him a while to formulate his escape strategy. The major challenge was getting over the first hurdle. He needed to start somewhere. He needed to fight his fears and get inside a vehicle. The more he agonised the more time would be lost. Eventually the need to get moving on his escape plan drove him onto a train. He chose that option as there was space; he could walk in the carriage if he became too anxious. Not that he had the foggiest clue if he would become flustered but he needed some reassurance.

His first objective was to spend time in Dublin. His research led to a few stores where he could walk in and buy the solvents he needed to process the castor oil beans. He also needed top quality protective gear, including breathing protection for working with the final results of his endeavours.

Mostly though, he wanted to get working on his planned escape travel itinerary which required quite a few steps to be in place before he would be ready for departure.

His basic plan required getting a passport. Then, when his Irish documents were in place, he would have to find someone who would help him lay his hands on a legitimate Taiwanese passport. The idea of a second identity brought a smile to his face,

"You're quite a canny bastard, now that you've got something to excite you!"

He silently admonished himself for muttering aloud. He knew the habit may land him in trouble but just as hard as it was to break a lifetime's fear of motorised travel so it was of breaking a habit of speaking aloud when he was on his own.

***

The train rattled along at a steady 70 miles per hour. John found himself relaxing more as every mile went by. At one point he silently admonished himself for not taking the plunge much sooner. The train's rhythmic motion soothed his fears to such an extent that he admitted he was actually enjoying the trip.

He stared out of the window at the coast below. This was easy, this would only make putting the rest of his plans together so much more enjoyable. Suddenly he realised that not many days previously he didn't know what he would be doing with himself but now he knew he would cherish every hour because each step along the new path made him feel so much more alive.

John's first impressions of Dublin were twofold; the speed at which things happened and the size of the place. It only took fifteen or so minutes to reach his first destination but by the time he arrived at the doors of *Mandarin for Everyone* he was flustered and realised he must be showing true country bumpkin signs of agitation. He kept going a few hundred meters, to settle his nerves, before returning and entering the Chinese Language School's doors.

He handed a copy of an e-mail to the attractive receptionist who pointed toward the stairs and informed him to turn left at the first floor landing and keep going until he reached Room 113. She would call ahead to inform Mrs Li that he was on his way.

Once seated, he explained his predicament to Mrs Li. He'd been offered a new role at work but it would require much travel in the East. He needed a firm grip on Mandarin but his time was very restricted. Could the school help him master the basics in little over two months? He would be more than happy to attend classes twice a week, for as long as it takes, for private lessons.

Mrs Li asked a few questions; would John be willing to visit the school for two three hour sessions on Tuesdays and Thursdays for the next eight weeks? Would he be prepared to do all his homework? Would he be willing to stay on if the tutors felt he needed more help after any particular session? Would he be willing to pay for half the lessons immediately?

Fifteen minutes later John was standing on the sidewalk again. He was quite amused at just how easy that was. The first basic element of his getaway was now beginning to take shape. He would become Chinese as soon as the need for his new identity arrived.

Yes, his mother would be proud if she could somehow know that he was returning to a distant past. He'd once asked her why he seemed to have more oriental facial features than western looks. He remembered her reluctance to answer, which at the time had made him wonder if maybe the wild stormy night in Bermuda was spent with someone other than his father.

She answered him a few days later. Without much ado she's made a passing remark about his Chinese grandmother. John pried about his past but he was left with very little. His father was a runaway orphan; she was the only daughter of an immigrant widow. They'd met in a dirty, rundown backstreet hotel in North London. He was the cook-cum-barkeep when she arrived to take the role of housekeeper.

At first they avoided each other but it didn't take long for the two of them to realise they were both lost souls in the wide ocean of humanity that was the population of a mega city. When her mother passed away she left her a few thousand Pounds, cash. That was enough for the two of them to get married. As she reminded him then, they went off to Bermuda, as he well knew by now.

His mother added that she loved his father. He'd used some of her inheritance to buy into the local pub in the seaside town when they settled in Ireland. He worked hard and by the time he sold on his share in the pub it was a thriving business. He cared well for them, promising her that as long as he lived she and Johnny B, as his father called him, would be well cared for.

The house, where he still lived, was bought by his father for a song, almost 40 years ago. With the profit made from the pub sale his father began buying and restoring houses. By the time he was killed he'd built up a sizable property portfolio. That portfolio kept them alive as his mother never worked after John was born. When his mother died a year ago she'd left him a sizable chunk of money for which he was grateful now. He would buy a new life for himself, yes that he would!

***

Two days later John completed his application for his first Irish passport. The very helpful lady at the post office guided him through the process. When he'd first called in to ask about all the required forms, she'd mentioned the photos.

"Remember to groom yourself because you want to look your best."

That gave him the idea to trim his beard down to a two week look. That would make it easier to regrow his beard for later travel, if he so desired. When he returned, freshly groomed, the woman didn't recognise him at first.

"My, you look so much younger with all that hair off your face!"

John made mental notes all the time. *Aha*, the art of changing your appearance to fit different situations was becoming an important strategy. More time needed on the finer details, he told himself. The devil is in the detail, or should that be the detail is in the devil? Yes, he'd be the most detailed devil he could be.

The biweekly train trips into Dublin soon became an enjoyable experience. However, his research into getting his hands on a valid Taiwanese passport was proving frustratingly fruitless. He realised a rank amateur like him stood little chance of obtaining a passport without expert help but how did he go about getting that help?

He needed a bit of luck if he was going to find the correct contact to help him in his search for a passport. His major concern with getting his Chinese identity in place was the need to move funds from his Irish accounts into some sort of offshore holding company in such a manner that there would be no apparent link between his identities.

An idea dawned halfway through his forth Mandarin lesson; he asked a seemingly random question.

"How would one change identity and obtain a Chinese passport?"

John was quite startled at the brazenness of his question; however, it seemed as if Mrs Li hadn't heard because she continued as if the question had never been asked. The lesson carried on as scheduled but as he was about to say his goodbyes the answer arrived.

"If you'd like some more information regarding your earlier question, be in reception at eleven thirty tomorrow morning. Ms Wang, our receptionist, will be expecting you. You may consider having a bit of money with you so I'd suggest visiting your bank before arriving."

With that the classroom door closed but the door to his future was allowed to squeak ajar just sufficiently to allow a ray of light to slip through.

John stood outside the door for what seemed an eternity. His mind was spinning. The seemingly ill-conceived question may just have been the key that unlocked the secret to his future. He shook his head, as if in disbelief and realised he needed to make a rather urgent phone call.

He thought for a second or two while scrolling down his contacts list. What would he say to Pete? He pressed call and waited the tense seconds for a response,

"Pete, John here… John Smith, yes, all's well. Sorry to disturb but would you be able to have twenty grand available for me tomorrow morning. Opening time please, I have a meeting to attend at eleven thirty for which I must be prepared. No, please don't ask now, I may be able to lay my hands on a distressed sale, yes; I need the deposit if I'm to succeed. Thanks, see you then… yes, I'll call in at nine thirty."

Phew, let's hope the man believes me, thought John. Fortunately, his bank manager was used to strange requests from the family. His mother would call him out of the blue to get her hands onto sums of money for investments. Occasionally the deals were dodgy but once in a while she would pull off something and within months happily replenish the account.

Right, thought John, now the fun was really beginning.

***

John was waiting at the bank when the doors opened. He was tired; sleep had evaded him most of the night, so he'd left the house early to grab a breakfast on route. He needed to calm his overactive mind and thought a healthy fry accompanied by a large pot of coffee would do the business.

The bank manager was waiting in his office and without much formality the funds were transferred across the desk. John spent a few minutes counting the notes. Once satisfied that all was correct he signed the release slip. He was already on the way toward the door when he realised he'd forgotten most of his manner in at the breakfast bar.

"Sorry Pete, please excuse my brash behaviour… my mind has been rather agitated by the whole deal so I've not slept a wink all night.

"Careful out there, don't put your money into anything too risky and if you need advice feel free to ring."

The concern on the bank man's face was genuine. John knew he was one of the good ones so he accepted the man's caution with a polite nod.

"Thanks Pete, I'll be careful and if all goes well I'll be back for more funds."

With that he closed the door and made his way out of the bank.

Within minutes John stepped into the waiting train carriage. His timing was good and his luck had held up well thus far, all good signs, he believed. He was hardly seated when he nodded off for what seemed only a few minutes. He woke to the sight of bright orange, the rail man in hi-vis jacket stood prodding at his shoulder.

"Sir, I have to ask you to leave the train, this is the last stop."

Recollection flooded back, John clutched at his laptop bag, relieved to feel it still safely stashed under his coat which he had draped over his legs before dozing off.

"Sorry, I'll leave now."

"No problem, I hope you enjoyed your morning snooze."

John anxiously looked at the time. Eleven ten. Twenty minutes to get to the language school. He glanced about. It dawned on him that he had missed his usual stop so he'd have to walk a few extra blocks but that wouldn't be too stressful as knew the route well enough by now.

John glanced at his watch before pressing the buzzer, eleven twenty eight. Phew, he made it with less than two minutes to spare. He heard the door latch releasing as the tinny intercom voice welcomed him in,

"Please enter Mr Smith, we're expecting you."

John paused a second or two for his eyes to adjust to the dim lighting in the reception area. The place was usually better lit when he attended classes so he wondered if they'd opened early specially for his visit. Ms Wang was waiting at the foot of the stairs; she tilted her head, beckoning him to follow. He made his way up the carpeted flight onto the first floor landing. Ms Wang pushed the second door on the right open and ushered him in. The door closed silently. He wondered if he'd heard the lock springing shut.

John had to pause again for his eyes to adjust to the semi darkness. The familiar voice of Mrs Li seemed to float at him from the corner of the room, as if the darkness separated their worlds.

"Welcome Mr Smith. With me is Michael Chen. Mr Chen is a negotiator of import and export contracts. If he cannot help you then no one can. Mr Chen, Mr Smith is seeking to lose himself by means of obtaining a Chinese identity, complete with a passport and other legitimate travel documentation."

John stood, speechlessly listening to Mrs Li's very perceptive summation of his unspoken wishes. This woman was far sharper that he'd given her credit for. She was most certainly not merely a language coach; that was becoming rather obvious with every sentence the woman spoke.

A thin, raspy voice joined in,

"I will not ask why, I will only ask when you plan to leave and if you ever plan to return?"

John thought for a minute or two. The second part of the question startled him slightly. He'd never even given it a thought. Honesty was what was required, he realised.

"I don't know; I've never really given it any thought. I've just recently obtained my Irish passport. I think… at the back of my mind I'd planned to have two separate identities. I'd chosen the bearded look for the Irish document. That will allow me to use the clean-shaven look for the Chinese identity."

"If you leave the country for good, you'll have to be able to live. That means money and the need for bank accounts. That means you'll need business connections for transferring funds. It's all good to get a passport for quick short-term travel but if you plan on never returning… you'll have to give serious thought to how you fund the rest of your life."

Silence descended, as if the pair of voices from the dark recesses of the room were purposely letting him stew in his own lukewarm juices. Maybe they thought that if they give him a minute or two to reflect, he'd turn on his heel and leave.

"I seem to have a few things to consider but I don't want to back down now."

"Ok," continued the raspy voice, "then we'll have to make a few decisions based on what your plans may be. Let's ask you a few more questions. You mentioned getting a new passport, have you ever travelled abroad?"

"No, I've only ever travelled in a train and only in the last month or so. I've always had a phobia for motorised transport so it's taken a bit of a leap of faith for me to even think of this new direction."

"You are single, aren't you?"

"Yes, since mom passed away I have no ties, here in Ireland or anywhere that I know of."

"Good, that makes it easier for us to create an identity that won't be easy to associate with John B Smith in the future."

John realised they must have done some sort of a background check on him. Easy, he thought, he'd given all his residential details when he'd enrolled for the classes. Not only that, he was paying for the lessons by debit order so they may even have been able to do a financial check as well. He had a fleeting thought that the alarm bells should be ringing but on the other hand, if they had the means to do checks then they must also be equipped to create this identity he was after.

"On the grounds of what you've said and the few bits of information we've put together we've come up with quite a simple plan. Mister Johnny Wang, as you said, you'll need to shave off that beard for your new identity photos."

John heard the faint click of the door lock unlatching behind him. Ms Wang entered and gestured for him to follow her. He trailed her to the bathroom where everything he needed was assembled on the dresser beside the double basins. Ms Wang pointed to the shaving gear and then took up a stool to the left to watch.

Fifteen minutes later they emerged from the bathroom. Ms Wang led him to a small study where she handed him a formal Chinese jacket and shirt. She gestured for him to change. While he was changing, she opened a desk drawer and fished about until finding what she was looking for.

"Here, put these on."

She handed him a pair of metal rimmed, traditional round glasses.

"Perfect, well, almost. I think you need to slick back your hair first. Come, back to the bathroom."

John followed meekly, as if bewitched by the attractive Chinese lady who's every word he was obeying.

He found gel on the dresser and after applying it he turned to Ms Wang for approval.

"Put on the glasses again and look at yourself in the mirror."

He did and was taken aback by the transformation. He didn't recognise himself so the chances of anyone else doing so would be rather slim.

"Come, we get your photos take."

Again, he followed in her silent wake.

Minutes later he was led back to the room where he'd met Mr Chen.

"I offer you Mr Johnny Wang."

This time Ms Wang stayed in the room.

"Aha… the two of you make a striking couple." Mr Chen's harsh nasal twang seemed to ram home what he'd just said.

"The Wang's?"

"Yes Mr Wang, you are going to need all the help you can get and Ms Wang here will be only too happy to be your coach and guide. She is long overdue a good holiday so please treat her with the necessary respect, from the moment you depart she will be your lifeline."

John stood in stunned silence. They had this all worked out before he even stepped through the door this morning. They were good, of that he was by now more than assured.

"Your passport and other documentation will be in order in a few days. You'll have a few bank accounts and cards that will enable you to move money about. For all of this you must leave fifteen thousand with us today."

John looked around for his laptop bag.

"You looking for this?"

Ms Wang stood with the bag dangling from the strap. He noted the faint smear of a smirk touching her delicate lips.

He reached for the bag as the thought dawned, he didn't have a clue what her name was.

"Ms Wang, if you are to be my guiding light, what should I call you?"

He smiled when he noticed the wink.

"Johnny Wang, I'm your woman, Lucy Wang."

"Charmed to meet you Lucy, I'm really looking forward to our adventure together."

Mr Chen's harsh shrill stopped any further light-hearted banter.

"Enough, we shall please continue. We'll have to establish the exact date of your departure and where you are planning to go. We need to get the itinerary worked out. Remember, you'll be a honeymoon couple so the details must be accurate."

John was suddenly conscious that he was still standing, still holding onto the laptop bag.

"I have the fifteen thou here…"

"Please pass the bag; I'll remove what's required."

Mrs Li appeared from the gloom to take the bag from John. He heard the door lock release and watched as Mrs Li left the room.

"You cannot return home for a few weeks as John Smith unless you want everyone in your hometown to find out about your subterfuge but I do want you and Lucy to put your disguise to the test and return there tomorrow, as the Wang's, for a sightseeing trip."

John found the challenge strangely exciting. The element of danger was enough to remind him of that enticing *alive* feeling he'd experienced lately.

Mr Chen must've seen a flicker of the excitement because he was quick to caution John,

"Careful, remember, your voice and mannerisms could easily give you away. You'll have to be very wary of where you go and how you approach what you do."

Mrs Li returned with the laptop bag.

"Just as well you came prepared. We suggest you sleep over tonight; Lucy will take you out for a bit of shopping and dinner. Tomorrow the two of you can drive down to Arklow for your outing."

***

The answer came to John some days later. He was standing at the water dispenser in a bank in the North. He noticed the patterned bands around the circumference of the large bottle. He had a closer look at the area where the label intersected the bands.

"Now, if I were to stick a hypodermic needle in under the label and then seal it somehow when I withdraw it… no one will ever see the mark!"

His discovery so excited him that he found himself muttering the words just about loud enough for the closest bystander to hear.

"Watch your big mouth," he cautioned himself, "at this rate you're bound to give yourself away!"

He was still standing deep in thought, elbow resting on the top of the bottle, when the bank manager called for him.

"Mr Smith, we have it all arranged for you now."

John followed the man into his offices. The man pointed at the bank draft documentation on his desk,

"Could I ask you to sign here please?"

He paused while John did as he was asked,

"And here, and then over the page… hold on, I'll show you."

Minutes later the banker handed him the bank draft,

"As requested by your man down in Arklow, a draft in the name of Three Pagoda's Investments."

John glanced at the details. All correct, including the figure. £435000.00. Yummy, he mumbled, the bankroll for the rest of his life was about to be established.

He thanked the man as he tucked the bank draft into the accompanying envelope. He placed the envelope into his laptop bag, which had become his carryall, turned on his heel, said his goodbyes and made his departure.

John walked into the coffee shop a block from the bank. He hesitated a few seconds to allow his eyes to adjust. He smiled when he spotted Lucy and made his way over to join her.

"Done, easy as pie."

"That calls for a bit of a celebration, don't you think?"

"Indeed Lucy, indeed. Let's finish up here and get out of Belfast. Have you managed to get another car?"

"Yes, using my *other* identity, no questions asked at all. We'll take a drive toward Letterkenny; we should get there before dark."

"It's going to take me a bit of getting used to, all this identity swapping."

"Don't worry, you'll soon be fully back to being Mr Smith, until we depart Ireland for the last time."

By the time they returned to Dublin a week later John was again looking like his old bearded self. After a Mandarin lesson with Mrs Li they met with Mr Chen. John handed over the bank draft. He hesitated a second or two; it was a lot of money to hand over to a stranger.

"Don't you trust me?"

The raspy, nasal voice cut through the gloom… and through his doubts.

"No sir, it's not a matter of trust, just a reluctance to part with so much money all in one go."

He hoped the lack of comment meant the man believed his lie.

"Rest assured, in two weeks' time you'll have your bank documents. Two separate accounts with different international banks as well as the necessary cards and pin codes."

John sighed, more out of relief than concern. Things were going well in his world. Now all he needed to do was go home, place his house on the market, make a plan to sell off his minor shareholding in the hell-hole of the company he was about to leave and put together the best part of the scheme.

His ricin plot!

***

John chose the summer solstice to harvest his crop of castor oil seeds.

He was out of the house by three in the morning, in the hope that he'd be able to get to the plants at first light and be away again before anyone had an inkling of what he was up to. He'd selected the plants well as the dense undergrowth shielded him from the potential of prying eyes.

The summer solstice. He looked on the date as an omen. The ancient Druids knew when to cast spells, they knew when to unleash their magic energies. He would harness the magic of the beans on this day of all days.

He was back home by five to begin the process of extracting the ricin from the beans. He carefully removed the outer casings of each bean. The task took forever but he felt this would be the best way to easily crush the beans. Bean by bean, minute by minute his pile of virgin white seeds grew. Another omen, he decided, removing the hard, protective casings to reveal the soft white internals of the beans.

John was so engrossed in his task that he didn't notice the time going by. He only realised how famished he was once he sat back to view his handiwork. Wow, ten past twelve. He'd been going far too long for comfort. Time for a break. However, he was keen to know how much raw material he had to work with.

He placed the bowl on the electronic scale. He sighed a contended sigh. Just over two kilograms. That would be enough to cook up enough magic. His magic.

Ok, he thought, quick shower and scrub, then out for another walk. A pub lunch would help. He'd considered all the options. While working the beans he'd eat out so as not to expose himself to any chances of inhaling or ingesting the toxin. First he placed all the husks into plastic bags. He would discard these in any of the conveniently placed bins in the town.

***

He sat outside, enjoying the warm summer sunshine. He chose to give himself a break after the first round of processing. He reflected on the progress to date. He'd obtained the chemicals on line without any hassles. The hydrochloric acid arrived from the UK a few days ago. He'd made up the first solution and washed the bean pulp a few times before filtration and neutralising the filtrate with sodium sulphate.

"Sir, you seem happy sitting out here in the lovely sunshine."

The waiter's untimely interruption brought John back to reality.

"Could I bring you another beer?"

"Yes please, that would be great."

John watched the man return into the dimness of the pub. He

turned his gaze outward again, outward to the water. The boats bobbed hypnotically on the gently flowing river. Subtle movement, just enough to sooth one into a state of calm. He enjoyed the feeling, as if his mind was already transported to foreign shores.

The man returned with the beer. John handed him a tenner and mutter for him to keep the change. The happy waiter went away whistling a vaguely familiar tune.

John's thoughts returned to the tasks still to be completed. The Ricin extraction was now getting to the tricky stages. He would soon have to begin working the cake. At that point all his precautions would come into effect. Chemical resistant suit, breathing apparatus, meticulous cleanliness and care taken with all the equipment.

It wasn't going to be easy putting on the suit alone but that wasn't the main issue. Getting it off without coming into contact with any ricin that may have contaminated the suit was going to be very risky. He realised he'd have to be at the top of his game and not lose sight of the dangers.

"In the shower, yes… that's it"

John's smile broadened at the thought of this Eureka moment. Yes, sitting here in the sun, enjoying the warmth and a cold beer, sure paid dividends. He glanced at the lowering sun before taking a final sip of beer. He slipped another tenner under the glass before leaving. He was halfway home before he realised he was humming the same tune the barman had been whistling.

Summertime... and the living's easy...

***

"How does he arrange all this stuff?"

John aired the question that had been churning in his head for a number of weeks. He glanced expectantly at Lucy, hoping for a satisfactory answer.

"My dear John, if I knew I would most likely be sworn to secrecy."

Her playful response brought a smile to John's worried face. He knew Lucy was toying with him but that made her even more endearing. He was conscious of another deeper emotion that seemed to be growing stronger every time they met. John's worried look must have returned.

"What's eating at you John, you seem particularly edgy today?"

How could he tell her what he was up to? How could he tell her why his tension was heightened? How could he tell her that within days he was going to put his revenge plan into motion? All he could do was suggest to Lucy that reason for his concern stemmed from his lack of understanding of how Mr Chen was managing to create his new identity.

"I just don't get how Mr Chen is doing it all. The passport, the bank accounts, money transfers, all while I do nothing but wait, nervously. What happens if his plans go wrong and I get caught at the airport next week?"

Lucy didn't answer immediately. She knew she'd have to reveal a few details to placate John.

"John, remember one thing, I'm in this with you. If you feel the pressure then surely I must feel the pressure too."

She hoped her approach would be sufficient. No, his expression didn't change much.

"Lucy, all you need to do is walk away if you see something going wrong. I'm sure you've done it all before so you'd know the signs. Remember, I'm totally at your mercy. I don't have a second crack at this. Once we're at the airport I've reached the point of no return."

"John, have you ever heard of the dark net?"

Lucy's hushed whisper startled John. Her tone turned icy.

"Have you?

His blank expression was sufficient answer.

"Let's go for a walk, St Stephens Green should be attractive today."

They rose silently. John instinctively knew he should keep his mouth shut until Lucy again indicated otherwise. Lucy paid on the way out. They stepped from the subdued interior of Bewley's into the bustle of Grafton Street. The two paused momentarily to allow their eyes to adjust to the bright sunlight.

Lucy hooked her arm into John's and led him toward the park. They passed by the Fusilier's Arch. Lucy chose to keep walking around the exterior of the park. Once they reached the much quieter gate on the south side she repeated her question.

"John, have you heard of the dark net?"

"No..."

"OK, it's the private web. It's where criminals contact each other. It's where unsavoury characters spread their filthy porn tentacles. It's where drug lords communicate with their minions but it is also where businessmen hang out when they want to make transactions difficult to trace. The dark net, together with the use of bitcoin has revolutionised money transfers."

Lucy paused when they arrived at the south east gate. She led John out of the park toward the Conrad Hotel on Earlsfort Terrace. Once inside the cool confines of the cocktail bar she made herself comfortable at John's side. She whispered in his ear, just like a lover would do.

"Our Mr Chen is a master of the dark net. I occasionally have to make connections for him but he is the driving force behind the operation. You chose well when you came to us with your request for a new identity."

Lucy playfully brushed his ear with her lips. She watched the confused expression spread across his face. She watched his blushes rising. Even in the subdued light she could see his awkwardness unfolding.

"John, I have to know. Next week this time we'll be on our honeymoon. Have you ever been with a woman or have you lived your whole life in the isolation you created for yourself?"

"No… never."

John's embarrassed reply only egged Lucy on.

"Oh John, my poor, poor man… we'll have to rectify that matter soon, won't we?"

Lucy winked at John, deepening his shade of scarlet a touch more.

"John, there's nothing to be worried about. I promise I won't hurt you."

John kept his mouth firmly shut. The fear of digging himself further into his own misery was only too obvious.

Lucy thought better of dragging out John's ordeal.

"What do you want to do for supper? Shall we remain here or go looking for something else?"

"The weather's still great outside. Why don't we go for a walk and then decide where to go? Anyway, I really enjoyed the place you took me the first time we went for dinner."

Lucy admired him for attempting to take the lead. She gave him a hurried peck on the cheek before getting up.

"Ok… lead on Mr Wang, lead on."

***

Four days after the summer solstice. Time was really running out for him now. By Friday afternoon he would have to be out of the country so the final few days needed rapid action. Their plane tickets had been secured. Mr and Mrs Wang would be flying out of Dublin International at 3:35 pm for Rio de Janeiro. In four days' time he would begin the best chapter of his life. The only chapter that mattered.

The jigsaw was coming together rapidly. The house sale had been completed during the weekend while he was in Dublin with Lucy. He didn't get the full asking price but then he didn't care that much either.

The e-mail from Sarah Moran in HR answered the four questions he has sent on.

Yes, the directors had decided to terminate his employment.

Yes, they would buy back his shareholding.

Yes, they would deposit the full-term service severance amount, together with the proceeds from the shares, into the account of Three Pagoda's Investments.

Last but not least, Sarah had arranged with Security to allow him to visit his office on Thursday evening.

John had asked if he could collect his effects in the evening when the offices were mostly deserted so he wouldn't have to answer any questions about his absence. Little did Sarah know that he would use the time to implement his plan.

John meticulously worked through the dismantling of the basic equipment he'd used to process his ricin. He'd used a coffee grinder to mill the filtered cake into the fine powder he required. This was the most difficult part of the operation. Once he'd successfully sealed the powder in Ziploc bags he placed everything in the shower. He turned on the shower and let it wash the items for a full five minutes before removing the respirator he was wearing and stepping into the shower himself.

The time had arrived for the final tasks. Getting rid of the chemical containers and equipment meant he needed to take a few strolls around the town. The containers were disposed of in the industrial bins down at the paint factory near the harbour. It suited him just fine that the bins were stored in a quiet lane outside the rear gates.

John dismantled the airtight Perspex box he'd used to contain the dust while milling the filtrate. The coffee grinder found a new home in the skip behind the Bay Hotel and the Perspex pieces unfortunately landed in a thicket along one of the forest paths to the west of the town. Bit by bit he disposed of all the evidence.

He wasn't going to make life easy for anyone who came looking for clues. The final task was to store the wooden chest he'd used to lock all his equipment and supplies away while the house was open for showing purposes. Getting it into the attic took a bit of doing but he eventually hoisted it in by throwing a rope over the roof truss above the trapdoor opening.

He contacted the estate agent on Thursday morning to find out if the sale proceedings were all in order. He passed on the details for Three Pagoda's Investments, instructing the woman to deposit the proceeds of the house sale into their account using his name as reference. He stressed that he would be out of town and would leave the keys to the front door with Mrs O'Malley at the post office.

The woman asked for a forwarding address but he told her he'd been let go at work and needed a break. He slipped in a throwaway comment about a ferry trip to the UK or the continent and not wanting to be bothered. Yes, he understood that the whole process could take a few months and no, he didn't mind how long it took.

John then went for a final walk down toward the harbour. He sat staring out across the river toward the sea. He played the whole routine through in his mind one last time.

Ricin had different effects on the human system, depending on how it was administered. If swallowed it would have the least effect so adding it to the water supplying the water fountains would make folk sick but most likely not kill anyone.

He knew exactly where all the water stations were located on the first floor. He would begin down at the western end of the floor where the managers and HR people congregated. It should not take him longer than ten minutes to inject a 100mm dose into each bottle. He may put in more or less; depending at what level he found each of the bottles.

His plan for that bitch Layla Mae was a little trickier. He had a two-pronged strategy for her. She loved exotic teas, so she always kept the flavour of the month at her desk. She loved smelling the tea so she would often just sniff at the bags or even at the contents of the open box.

She also suffered the unsightly effects of vesiculo-erosive skin disease. He knew the term off-hand because he'd heard her explain a million times why her arms were often covered in raw sores and blisters. She was constantly smearing E45 onto her arms so she always kept a tub or two of the grease close at hand.

He needed Lady Luck to be on his side in getting the ricin into her. He needed both the containers to be as full as possible. He planned to add about 15 grams of toxin to the tea and 25 grams to the cream. If all went to plan the ricin would start working anywhere between 24 and 48 hours after being ingested.

In the case of the beloved bitch Layla Mae it would most likely be a bit sooner but as she only started work at 09h30 he should be on the plane before she took ill. The thought of being on the plane with Lucy quickened his pulse. He wondered about the heightened feeling of anticipation at the mere thought of being with her.

"No… don't get yourself distracted at this point in time!"

His self-reprimand was enough to force his thoughts back to the events that would unfold in the next 24 hours. Soon he'd return home to collect his bag of tricks. Not long after that and he'd be heading to work, for the second last time.

Alive! That feeling of excitement overtook him again. The adrenalin levels must be up again, he thought. Between the excitement of his plot and the growing feelings for Lucy he realised that life could be rewarding. Yes, his brand new life was about to begin!

Once his mission was completed on this eventful night, he needed only one further unpleasant visit to his place of work for the meeting with Sarah from HR. That would be the last task. After that he'd set off for the airport. The prearranged taxi would be waiting. All he'd have with him would be the bag Mr Chen had asked him to pack, the diversionary bag.

All his plans were in place. Everything was as ready as it would ever be. He sat staring out at the boats bobbing on the rising tide. He would never sit here again, well, not as John Bermuda Smith. OK, Johnny B, he muttered, time for the final play to begin.

***

John made a simple airtight fume hood to contain any ricin dust that may spill when he transferred the powder into the water. He'd placed the open bottle in a large clear plastic bag along with the sealed 50 gram bag of ricin powder. Once he was happy with his preparations, he sealed the bag by knotting the open end.

He worked very carefully through the membrane of the bag. He wore the respirator as an additional precaution but all went well. He managed to open the Ziploc bag and poured the powder into the water without spilling any ricin. He replaced the screw top and tightened it as much as possible without tearing the outer bag. Then he switched on the vacuum cleaner and plunged his homemade metal nozzle into the bag.

He watched as the bag collapsed before pulling out the nozzle and switching off the machine. He carefully removed the bottle from the deflated bag. Fortunately, as he had hoped, the empty Ziploc bag had been sucked up by the vacuum cleaner. He tightened the bottle top before shaking the contents vigorously. When he was satisfied that the powder had properly dissolved the bottle joined the other bits of kit in the bag. A waterproof apron, two 100mm syringes together with needles and a new, sealed respirator. The two remaining bags of ricin powder were stored in a cotton wool lined cigar case.

John checked the carryall a second time. What was missing? Gloves! He added two chemical resistant pairs as well as a few spatulas for mixing the ricin into the cream. He ran through the plan in his head one more time before setting off to his place of work at 8:30 pm.

Liam at the Main Gate Security was only too happy to allow John in. They chatted briefly about the happenings of the past few months. Liam's questioned what he'd been up to during his sabbatical. Aha, thought John, that was the line HR had run with. Sabbatical, my posterior!

John donned a pair of gloves when he reached his desk. He removed the two syringes, fitted a needle to each and gave his ricin solution bottle another shake. He carefully removed the lid and filled the two syringes. Then he casually strolled to the water station just beside the HR desks. The bottle was just over half full. He peeled the label away slightly before plunging the needle into the plastic just above the water line.

He didn't hesitate a second. There was that alive feeling again. He emptied the full 100mm into the bottle, withdrew the needle and flattened out the label, in so doing hiding the small puncture. He moved to the next water station and repeated the exercise.

He drained the contents of the ricin water within minutes. He slipped the two syringes into the confidential waste bins. He knew it would be weeks before the bins were collected for emptying. John felt his smile broadening. The syringes stood a good chance of being incinerated without ever being found.

He returned to his desk and attempted to log on to his PC. No such luck. He'd been locked out, just as he thought. He breathed a sigh, a contented sigh at that. OK Johnny boy, get this over and done with, won't you?

John walked into Layla Mae's cubicle. He stood for a second, looking at the layout of her desk. He took particular notice of the two items he was after. He used his phone to take a few reference photos before picking up the tea box and the open tub of cream.

John walked to the nearest men's toilets. He locked himself into one of the stalls before putting on his protective gear. First the apron and then the second pair of gloves. Then he removed the new respirator and ensured the filters were correctly installed. He donned the contraption, ensuring that the face seal was as tight as he could make it.

He sat down on the toilet seat for a few moments. He needed a quick breather to restore his calm. He knew he was tense and didn't want the tension to interfere with his actions at this important part of proceedings. All he needed now was to mess up and all his hard work would be undone at the last moment.

Ten minutes later the job was complete. The tub of cream was almost full so he'd poured in the powder and carefully mixed the contents for a few minutes. Then he'd emptied the last bag of powder all over the tea bags. This was going to be the difficult one to pull off. He needed the powder to stick so he tapped at each bag individually in the hope that the powder was fine enough to pass through the pores in the bags. His efforts seemed to work so when he was satisfied with the results he closed the lid as tightly as possible.

He removed all the protective gear very carefully. He hoped he wasn't breathing in any residual dust that may still be suspended in the air. He bagged the apron, gloves and respirator and returned to his office. He relaxed in his chair for a few minutes before returning the tea and cream to their precise locations on Layla Mae's desk. He double checked the positions and stood back to compare his handiwork with the photos.

John placed the used equipment in one of the chemical contamination disposal bins near the factory door on the ground floor before returning to his cubicle to clear out his last few possessions.

He felt drained. He needed to get out so he packed his few things in the bag and made his way toward the site exit. Liam wanted John to stay around for a few minutes but John declined. He'd had enough of the place and couldn't wait to get his last visit out of the way in the morning.

***

Sarah Moran was waiting in Reception when he arrived at ten. She ushered him into the interview room closest to the exit. There was very little interaction and that pleased John. He was in no mood to make idle chatter on a morning like this. He'd not really slept at all and now being so close to the scene of last night's efforts put him further on edge.

Sarah mistook his mood for sadness and muttered something about things not being all bad. How far from the truth could she be, he wondered? All the documentation was signed within minutes. He was about to rise when Sarah gestured for him to stay seated.

"Wait a second, I will ring payroll to action the funds transfer immediately. Also, Gerry wants to pop in. Why now, wondered John? Why did the MD now want to meet with him?

Sarah made the two brief phone calls.

"Gerry is on his way and your funds are being transferred as we speak."

Gerry arrived a minute later. He greeted John and spoke briefly about the difficult decision the board had to make. John remained silent. He really wanted to get out of the place in a hurry and get to the unmarked taxi that was waiting a block away.

Gerry noticed John's unresponsiveness and cut short what he was saying.

"Sorry, I think you must be anxious to get out of here. I suppose I'd be the same if I were in your shoes so let me walk you to the door."

John was sure his relief showed but he didn't care, he would be on his way to his new life within minutes.

***

John smiled as he read the Irish Times online article.

"An Garda Siochana have lodged a formal request for assistance with Scotland Yard. They are seeking the assistance of a Mr John Smith in relation to what is believed to be a poison attack at the Arklow Chemicals Company. A number of employees, believed to be as many as 31, may have suffered the effects of the poisoning."

John paused. Yes, that would be about correct. Pity a few more didn't get a wakeup call. He glanced further down the page. Yep, there it was.

"Further reports suggest that one employee suffered critical complications. Miss Layla Mae McCabe was reported to be out of intensive care and in a stable condition. However, doctors fear she may suffer side effects for the rest of her life."

"It is believed Mr Smith boarded a ferry in Rosslare last Friday evening. A bag containing Mr Smith's personal effects was recovered at the ferry terminal in Fishgaurd earlier this week."

"Witnesses have said it was difficult to come to terms with the events because they all knew Mr Smith as a very private, harmless character who had apparently accepted a severance package after 25 years of service just before the attack took place."

"Anyone with any information is asked to contact the Arklow Garda Station or the Crime Stop free call number."

John put the tablet down on the coffee table. He couldn't get rid of the smile on his face. Some severance package! He had gained so much - including his freedom and newfound sense of adventure.

Yet, thankfully, he had lost much as well, including his phobias and fears but most of all, his virginity - to the woman who lay snuggled up beside him.

Now, here's the Thing!

"You only back in today then?"

"Yeah man, had a serious run of the dose, stayed in bed the whole weekend."

"Bummer! Don't you just hate that? Bust yer arse off all week in this dump then when you wanna go on the tear you land up full of the dose and have to stay in. Serves you right to stay home on a Monday."

"Fek man, didn't want to stay home, I hate losing pay but I had to, sick as a small hospital, I was."

"You don't sound over it yet."

"No, but I'll get by with a few Sippy Lem's."

Silence descended for a few seconds. Neither man willing to continue the conversation. Pete poked at the last sausage on his plate.

"The fry is good today."

"You think so? My taste buds are so numb that it all tastes the same to me. Must be the dose that's affected my senses."

"Ah yes, I get that way too when I'm sick, then everything tastes like cardboard."

"Big brother."

"What?" Pete's startled expression only served to entice more of the same.

"Big Brother, that's what I said. Big brother is to blame for all this shite!"

Pete sat back in his chair, shaking his head slowly from side to side. He wondered if his friend had lost the plot.

"Now, here's a thing..."

"You lost it? Here's what?

"A thing, says I. Not a thing of beauty either!"

Pete stared at the man across the table. He wasn't sure if he should waste any more words on this conversation and was about to leave. He glanced at his watch and thought he'd stay for a few minutes longer. Maybe the man needed talk.

"Have you ever wondered who's to benefit when we're ill?"

"No? Why should I wonder about shite like that?"

"You gotta stop and think man; they're doing it to us."

"They?"

"Big brother..."

Now Pete was convinced of his mate's brain fade.

"Ah come on man, you get a bit of the dose and get back to work reformed into some sort of doomsday prophet. You been chewing your socks or something?"

"No, listen. Here's the thing."

Pete's exasperation reached breaking point.

"Ah fek man, if you say '*now here's the thing*' again I'll be likely to slap the shite outta you!"

"No! Wait... I'll explain. Sit a little; you'll soon see what I'm getting at."

He reached inside his pocket and scratched around for a few seconds before producing the sachet he was searching for.

"You see this Sippy Lem? How many of these do you usually take before they seem to get a hold of your dose?"

Pete paused for a moment, "I don't know… three, no more usually. So, what's the point?"

"How many do they put in the box?"

"Five, I think..."

"Aha! Now, do you see where're I heading?"

"No man, what's the amount of sachets in the box got to do with your big brother theory?"

"Think man, use your head. So if there's five in the box and you need about that many you'll get two boxes at a time, won't you?"

Pete looked at the man's strange expression before replying.

"I suppose so but hey, that still doesn't spell danger, does it?"

"OK, look at it this way, one sachet doesn't seem to give you much relief. You're usually so full of the dose that it feels you need another within two hours of the first. So you take another one. That leaves you with 3 in the box. Now, before you're even remotely better you need another."

He paused for a sip of tea.

"Now you're getting desperate, you'd better call for more or if there's no one home you'd better drag yourself through the shower, get dressed and go get your own replenishment."

"Yes, yes and yes again. I've been there but I still don't see how world domination comes in a box of Sippy Lem's"

"What's a box cost? About €4 at your local store."

"So, that's a whole lot cheaper than paying a doctor 50 quid for a visit. Then he writes you a script that could well set you back more than 20 at the pharmacy. For me, two boxes of Sippy Lem is always the winner."

"OK, here's the thing..."

"Ah, there you go again. What's the thing this time?"

"Think man, think. They want you to have more than one box. So, you get at least two. That sets you back well over € 8. What would you

say it costs to make one sachet? Ten cents? Let's say, with all costs involved a box gets onto the shelves for about three euros. The storekeeper makes a good bit of profit which is of course taxed to the hilt."

Pete thought he was getting the drift now.

"So, everyone pays their dues to the government? Is that what you're getting at?"

"Well, well, well, you've eventually woken up. Yes, you're getting warm. That's the beginning of the tale."

Pete sighed, an extended escape of frustrated air.

"OK, we all pay taxes but how does that get big brother into the equation?"

"The pharma companies are a law unto themselves. They set prices however that want to. Next, the government takes its massive slice."

"Oh come on, quit the crap and get to the big brother angle, won't you?"

"There's a pattern, you have to understand the pattern to see how it all fits together. They want us sick, they don't want us well. We're worth a lot more ill than well."

"Grand, they make a few bob off our misery but surely that doesn't lead to world domination."

Pete's irritation grew with every sentence.

"How do you see a pattern developing?"

"Easy, if we're ill the pharma companies cream the profits off the top. The big players, they unite with the even bigger moguls to plot. They spray us with chemicals, with manmade viruses. You heard of con trails?"

"Aaaak fek! Now you're really asking me to believe the impossible. I'm going, I've had enough of this shite!"

Pete pushed back his chair and was about to get up when *that* phrase stopped him in his tracks.

"Now here's the thing..."

"WHAT THING!"

"Summer flus, winter infections, autumn viral strains... pig sicknesses, fowl flus, even in the spring we rush out to get the Sippy Lem's. Why are we always ill? Because they want us to be ill!"

"OK, you've made your point; they want us to be ill, however, help me out here, why?"

"Now we're getting close. They rule our every existence; they even plan our illnesses. They want us weak so we don't rise to challenge."

"Hold on, who's they? You keep prattling on about them but you don't say who they are. Surely it's not the pharma companies or the government who're to blame?"

"You're right, it's the masterminds. The very few mega rich, the master rulers who play the pharma industry and pitiful little governments like puppets."

"So, you're saying that even if the taxman loses when you don't work a day they still win?"

"Yes, of course! The more sachets of the stuff they sell the better for them. They don't worry too much about the profits; they worry more about the outcome."

Pete watched in stunned silence. His pal must've chewed mushrooms or smoked laced pot while he was out sick. Here's a man, who last week was an ordinary fella, who'd now turned into a doomsday prophet.

"So, you have a few sachets of powder and you feel better after a few days, all well. A few bob goes here; a few bob goes there. So what?"

"Look man, don't you see. They've included other active ingredients in the mix. These others accumulate in the body. Now, you begin feeling better but just so you don't have a relapse you have one or two more. That's just what they want you to do."

"Yes," signed Pete again, "of course they want to make more profit…"

"And, they want you to ingest more of the other ingredients. Soon your insides turn tender. Yep, the crapper will call. Often. That's the pattern taking shape."

"Now here's a thing…" Pete's mockingly pre-empted, "Who would have guessed? They planned it that way… so you shite your lungs out just as you thought you were getting better."

"Exactly!"

Pete stuck out his hand in an attempt to stop what was coming next. To no avail.

"Now, here's a thing... now you have to go off to the pharmacy to get something for cramp and something to plug the hole. Yep, the corner store isn't authorised to stock these desperately needed cures."

"All good and well, we've gone from sorting out our colds to having the runs, we've not quite arrived at total world domination, have we?"

"No, but we're almost there. The mega masters have it all mapped out. You get your latest batch of stuff from the pharmacy, then, before you know it you need something to remove the plug because the

heartburn is killing you."

"Now, here's the thing." Pete added for effect.

"Yes, indeed, here's the thing... all these chemicals we're throwing down our throats have consequences. The mega masters make more money, grab more companies, rig more elections and gain more control. Yes, all at the expense of our health!"

Pete sighed one last time and slowly rose.

"Enough!"

He turned on his heel and strode away without managing to escape the words...

"Now, here's the thing, all these chemical cocktails induce life threatening diseases like cancers and neurological disorders, needing more interventions..."

Oh damn... he thought, all for the price of a few sachets of Sippy Lem!

The Blaster's Daughter

Zach was waiting at one of the old concrete picnic tables, once a feature at the lowest point of the *poort*, close to where the road crossed the river. The tall, dark stranger with the piercing blue eyes must be his contact, Willie Berg, the local guide and historian.

He'd come to know of Willie's fame months back while researching the impact of construction projects on the folklore of rural areas. The idea of using this as a focus for his honours thesis stemmed from fascination with the Bain's Kloof Ghost. He'd realised that the tales of myth and mystery were often only known to a few in the community. He'd also realised that the local legends usually began during an event of upheaval such as the construction of a road or dam.

Willie extended a welcoming hand as soon as he was within reach. His thick Karoo accent brought a smile to Zach. Was Willie putting on a show or was he for real? Zach realised within minutes that the man was for real. His laid-back manner hardly suppressed the infectious enthusiasm welling from his craving to have the area's history documented in every way possible.

The men chatted about Zach's mission and how Willie could assist. Yes, there was a very real tale here. The Meirings Poort history was dotted with happenings of note, none more so than the tale of the blaster who played a part in the road upgrade works of the late forties.

"Ask away Zach… I'll fill in the details."

"Great," enthused Zach, *"let's begin with the building of the first pass through the poort."*

"Ja ok, the main story you're actually after happened much later but let's begin with that first project. The original pass was constructed in the late 1850's. One of the famous Bain brothers was the engineer, you know… the Bain's who built the passes nearer to Cape Town…"

Willie paused when he noticed Zach's expression. He couldn't quite make out the look in Zach's eyes… pained exhilaration? Perplexed euphoria?

"Don't I just know?" He paused, momentarily reflecting on his past brush with the supernatural, *"Yes, it's the story of the so-called Ghost of Bain's Kloof that really got me interested in these fables."*

Zach's calm exterior and matter of fact tone belied the stirrings within. The effect *that* ghost has on him… the mere mention of her was usually enough to agitate strange forces in his soul.

"I'll tell you what, those were difficult days." Willie paused, wiped his brow with the back of his hand, flicked the sweat off

nonchalantly, before replacing his stained felt hat.

"Those were days when hard men died like flies in the heat and rock falls."

Willie paused again. He looked about, as if he was expecting to see something or someone appear while they waited.

"Look over there..." he pointed toward a jagged, rather strange looking outcrop, *"can you see boulders? The sunlight is just falling nicely on them now..."*

"Aha," thought Zack, *"that's why Willie suggested we meet at this time of the day."*

The oppressive summer heat was at its worst as the sun finally made its way far enough west to be able to throw direct light on the steep walls of the rock face.

"Die klippe praat... ja, hier vertel die klippe stories!"

Zach mumbled the words... as if entranced, *"The rocks talk... yes, here the rocks tell tales..."*

He looked again at the rocky outcrop. Was he seeing things or did it appear to be the profile of a person? Was he right? Did it seem as if the tumbling rocks had come gently to rest on a body and in so doing taken on the outline of the shape beneath?

No, his imagination was messing with his mind again. He kept his eyes firmly fixed on the pile of jagged rocks as Willie chatted on.

"That pile of rocks is the visible manifestation of the story which in these parts is passed from generation to generation in whispered mutters. So much of the story is shrouded in secrecy as too many of the facts were hidden from the authorities because of their implications." Willie paused, again removing his hat to wipe the sweat from his brow.

"Come, we find shade... you've seen the rock pile so there's no need to let Uncle Spikes dart his rays directly into us."

He led Zack in the direction of a shady knoll where a picnic basket was waiting atop one of the newer wooden tables.

"Please make yourself comfortable... a glass of wine? Local, robust red berry nectar."

Willie removed the bottle from the cooler box beneath the table, flipped over the glasses, glanced in Zack's direction before pouring.

"Thanks, you seem to have thought of everything."

"My pleasure... we have a few hours to while away so we may as well make the best of the restful surroundings."

Willie passed over a glass of the chilled red wine. The two men raised a silent toast, each immersed in their own thoughts. Zack wondered where this was leading. He'd waited months for this meeting, now here they were sitting in silence.

"The Blaster's daughter..."

The words seemed to crackle in the air. Did Zach sense an edge to Willie's tone? Was there an underlying torrent waiting to spew from a hidden geyser of emotion?

"The Blaster's daughter."

The repeated words held less menace the second time, as if the crackle had been discharged, the static released back into the ether.

***

Willie gently shook Zack's shoulder, *"Zack, wake up before you miss the moon rise."*

Zack sat bolt upright, it took him a few seconds to recollect where he was and what had transpired that afternoon. He looked around; the twilight was setting in even as he recalled Willie's tale.

"In those days, not long after the war, folk here in the platteland still did things in the old ways. Local labour was often used during the projects but as you are well aware, additional labour is always necessary when larger projects get going."

Zack recalled sitting, sipping at his wine and occasionally taking a bite of cheese or cold meat. The wine was robust but good none-the-less. However, together with oppressive summer heat, it was making him drowsy. Willie noticed his eyelids drooping.

"Relax there; I have a blanket to throw down on the grass so you don't itch..."

Willie pointed in the direction of a shady spot of lawn beneath a gnarled old Karee tree. He noticed Zach's reaction and spoke before Zack could open his mouth.

"Have a lie down there, don't worry, I'll make sure you won't miss a thing."

"But... but," Zach stammered in half protest, *"I'll miss the story"*

"No, I'll fill you in while you're resting."

Willie went on to tell of the big German who'd settled in the area not long after World War One. *The Blaster,* he'd soon become known as. He was a man of few words and much action. He'd soon earned enough to acquire a small bit of land and build a cottage for himself.

"Some say he was a loner who chose to live the life of solitude, some say he'd run away from the scars of the horrors of the war. Anyway, seemingly he only ever befriended one person. A young local girl. It was before the days of apartheid and even though mixed marriages were frowned on they were not against the law in those days."

Zach recalled Willie's words, wondering how he could because he thought he'd dozed off moments after making himself comfortable on the blanket.

"Apparently, the tiny woman died of complications after the birth of their first child. The Blaster raised his daughter single handed, always taking her along when he went working on distant projects. He schooled her when they were away. She grew up basically only knowing the man who was her father."

At that point Willie had paused to pour a little more wine. Zach recalled opening one eye to see the man having a slow sip which had in turn made him sit up and reach for his glass. It was empty but Willie stepped over to top it up.

A strange feeling crept over Zach. Was the wine doctored? Did it put him in a trance like slumber? No, surely Willie would've been affected in the same way.

Willie resumed the tale as soon as Zach again settled down.

"Then, the authorities made the funds available for the upgrades to Meirings Poort. The Blaster was in his element. He could settle at home for an extended period of time. His daughter was by now a lovely young lady who'd blossomed into an attractive, tall athletic teenager. Needless to say, the old Blaster was fiercely protective of the young lady."

Again Zach wondered if he'd dreamed the tale or if he'd been sufficiently conscious to take in Willie's melodic recounting of the story. Was it the wine or the hypnotic tones of a seer that had this effect on him? Was he being slightly paranoid? It mattered little… he could feel the warm tingle of the unexpected creeping up his spine, even as dread's cold sweat trickled slowly downward along the same path.

"Tell me more, do tell me more…" was all he could stutter.

"Relax, I will…" Willie replied.

There's that word again, relax. Was that the trigger word setting off his strange feeling of suspension? Zach shook his head, as if to rid himself of the cobwebs of slumber spun in the recesses of his mind. *Relax.*

"The Blaster was one of the main men on the project, often arranging the work parties along the construction route. This is how most of the folk along the way got to know of the attractive young lady who always accompanied him. Unfortunately, this was also the beginning of the trouble. One of the work parties comprised ex World War Two German POW's who often chatted freely when the Blaster and his daughter passed their way."

"Inevitably, the Blaster broke one of his unspoken rules and invited two brothers to his cottage. The men visited often. The Blaster

wanted to know about the war and about Germany, he wanted his daughter to get an inkling of the old land."

"Slowly but surely he dropped his guard and on the odd occasion would even allow the girl to go off to the camp shop with one or both of the brothers to buy supplies. On one of these fateful trips the men took advantage of the girl's trust and friendship. Her innocence was shattered, her soul scarred forever."

"The old Blaster was heartbroken when he realised his daughter was pregnant. The men denied all wrong doing, blaming the girl for seducing them. However, the girl was strangely content with her lot, eventually convincing the old man that it was meant to be. She cherished the new life growing inside her."

Zach sat staring into space. It was as if every word was recorded forever on an indelible memory device slotted into the subconscious recesses of his mind.

"Surely there must be more to the story Willie, something that I don't quite understand, why did you insist I visit you on this day? I've been waiting months for this opportunity."

Zach looked over at Willie. All he noticed was a radiant smile and the twinkle in the piercing blue eyes, as if Willie had been expectantly waiting for this day all his life.

"Aha, this day is the summer solstice; it's also a very rare summer solstice, full moon this evening. I wanted you to see the rock pile in the afternoon when fully illuminated by the sun. As I've mentioned, it's believed to be the burial mound of the two German's who were to blame for Blaster's daughter's ordeal."

Willie paused at this point to again top up their glasses. Each sat with their thoughts for a minute or so while slowly sipping the rich red essence of the earth.

"Soon the moon will be rising... soon the whole tale will be revealed. Before that happens I'll complete the story of the Blaster. "

Willie glanced over in Zach's direction, as if to see if he had his full attention.

"The Blaster accepted the fate of his daughter's pregnancy, he even stopped ranting about the two brother's lack of respect for breaking the trust he'd placed in them. However, as was the case when his wife died in childbirth, his beautiful daughter also didn't survive the ordeal. The Blaster was left with not only the baby but an inconsolable grief."

This time Willie noted Zach's wide-eyed surprise, enough encouragement for him to press on.

"Some say the Blaster lost his mind, some say his loss was so

great he had to find an outlet for his anger and sorrow. Some asked after the incident if the two brothers didn't just flee. No, the rumour persisted, he'd set the dynamite, then lured the brothers onto the rock face and then blasted it off, trapping them in the resulting rock fall. Too neat? Many won't believe that the old man was capable of doing such a deed. They say he simply banished the men. The old folk say he..."

Zach raised his hand, stopping Willie in mid-sentence,

"If that was the end of the tale you wouldn't have made me wait this long... or travel this far for such a weak ending."

Zach's matter-of-fact statement didn't escape Willie.

"No, I wouldn't have done that."

"Come on man! Spill the beans, I've waited too long to hear the full story!"

"Relax Zach, just a little more patience! "

"You still haven't explained the significance of the summer solstice..."

"Oh yes, sorry... the child was born on the solstice, his mother died the same evening. The old folk say you can see the Blaster's daughter on the full moon closest to the southern summer date. However, it is rumoured that she only shows herself when the full moon coincides with the solstice."

Willie's flat, monotone recounting seemed more of a chant than a story, a druid's chant!

"Wow... that will be some happening!"

Zach's anticipation was reaching new heights; he couldn't contain his excitement any longer.

"Rise moon, rise! I want to see her!"

The ensuing pause and silence between the men seemed to drag on for an eternity. Eventually Willie broke the silence,

"Come, the moon will soon be making its appearance so let's get into position. We have to be in the correct spot, we have to place the burial pile between us and the rising moon."

Willie set off without as much of another glance in Zach's direction. He was a man on a very deliberate mission.

Zach hurriedly followed, only catching up with Willie as he stopped and turned to see if he was in the correct spot. Zach had the unmistaken feeling that Willie knew exactly where the exact spot was, as if he'd frequented this bit of earth many times in the past.

"This is the spot... we wait."

Willie's whispered tone turned business-like, no longer the harmonic story teller or the druid's chant.

"You'll first see faint misty swirls against the moon's glow...

almost like the effects of a heat haze... you know, when you see the shimmer in the midday heat. Some say it's just the thermal energy released by the warm rocks... I know better."

The last portion of the sentence was snapped off in staccato fashion by a man who was at this stage not even realising he was speaking.

Zach questioned in a hushed tone,

"What will we see next?"

"Quiet!" Snapped Willie, *"You'll scare her away... be quiet!"*

"The shimmer will become clearer... see, there she is!"

Zach stood beside Willie; the cold shiver raised the hairs at the base of his neck. Slowly but surely, he could discern the shape of a woman hovering inches above the rock pile.

"Look at her beauty... look, can you see her?"

"Yes... yes, she's absolutely stunning... look at her twirling... "

Zach's hushed whisper trailed off, the two men watched in spellbound wonder as the lithe figure gyrated against the backdrop of the full honey moon. Ethereal dizzying beauty!

The men watched the silent swaying of sorrow upon the rocks. Slowly, very slowly, as the moon rose the figure of the Blaster's daughter rose. Then Zach realised he was hearing a strange wailing whimper beside him. He dared not look at Willie for fear of losing sight of the beautiful creature ahead but the soft wailing only enhanced the exhilarating horror of the moment.

"Don't leave me..."

Willie's panted whispers seemed to be wrenched from deep within, as if the figure was tearing chunks of his soul from him.

"Don't leave," he sobbed, "don't desert me again... please mamma... don't go again!"

"Please Mamma!"

Festival of the Two Moon Rising

There was that look again. No, that wasn't a look; it was a kaleidoscope of swirling colour. The turquoise flecks seemed to dance against the background of neon emerald. Her eyes seemed far too large for her scull but that just seemed to be an illusion. Each time she glanced rearward the eyes would further mesmerise… further entice… further strengthen the spell she was casting.

He hurried along, somehow finding the energy to keep up. He noticed his strides were longer, as if he was bounding along rather than walking. Brisk was the progress yet he sensed the figure leading him on was getting more impatient with each rearward glance.

"Come on Barnabas, we have to make haste."

Whoever calls him Barnabas these days? Anyhow, who was she and how did she know his name in the first place?

"Who are you? Why am I following you?"

"I'm Earth Mother, that's who I am."

Barny's confusion grew with each word Earth Mother spoke. He was convinced he heard birdsong yet he understood each word. Her beautifully lilting voice cut through the sounds of the undergrowth with a surreally unnatural clarity.

"Who are you?"

"Don't you believe me? I'm Earth Mother, simple."

"Ok Earth Mother, where am I? What am I doing here? Where am I going? Why is your hair like a floral meadow? Is your skin as smooth as it seems? Why am I dreaming this?"

"Take it easy earthling; your impatience is so representative of the ills of your race. Calm down, all will be revealed... soon."

He followed as best he could. Keeping up was becoming more difficult with each passing hour, or that's how it seemed to him. Surely he must have been running after the creature for most of the day. Day? He wondered about that? No sign of a sun or of a direct light source. There seemed to be no sky or shadows yet he could see everything clearly. Wherever he looked the trees disappeared into the low swirling mists.

"Earth Mother?"

No reply, just the soft sounds of the swirling vapours wrapping around everything in sight. He tried again, a little more forcefully.

"Earth Mother?"

"Yes child? What vexes you this time?"

"Please tell me where we are? Where am I? Are you real? Am I real? Is this place real?"

"Patience child, all will become clearer before too long. We must keep going otherwise we're not going to get there in time."

"Get where?"

"To the Two Moon Rising Festival, that's where. We're going to miss the start if you can't keep up. We'll have to get a move on or get you some help."

Earth Mother stopped so unexpectedly that he crashed into her. The impact sent him flying. In that moment he knew she was real. How else could this all be happening if he'd not just touched one of the most beautiful creatures imaginable? Surely, if she was an apparition, he'd not have been flung to the ground!

He looked up at the tall woman standing over him. Yes, she must be a woman even though she was unlike any other female of his species. Her hair seemed to form a cloud around her head and shoulders. Each floret entwined strand ending with minute colourful, daisy like flowers. And those eyes! The kaleidoscopes swirled constantly. The shades and hues changed unceasingly.

"Up with you."

He reached for her extended hand. This time the contact was gently invigorating. He felt a surge through his veins as she pulled him upwards. Blasts of adrenalin shot though his tired body. He stared at her beauty. Her close proximity, while she helped him to his feet, unnerved him even more. The almost translucent pale mint green of her skin enhanced the striking mauve of her delicate lips.

Her layered dress of leaves rustled gently as she moved, lulling him into an even deeper trance. Mixed sensations heightened his awareness. He sensed rather than saw her shapely figure beneath the dress. Yet, at times it seemed he could almost see through the covering… almost. He felt himself blushing at the idea of being aroused by rustling leaves. What was happening to him?

"Come child, you've seen enough. We must get going again. You can't let your mind drift, it will only lead to trouble."

Barny realised she was looking into his mind; she was reading his thoughts almost before he was aware of them. Oh well, he thought, he couldn't win this one so he may as well take the liberty of one last longing look before she turned and moved off again. Yes, the vision would be emblazoned onto his soul forever.

"You must not let your thoughts and ideas ruin your purpose here; you cannot let the frailties of earthlings skew your reason… that would be wrong."

"Earth Mother, where am I? Please tell me? Please tell me how I got here? Please."

"You are learning... patience will reveal the answers to those who wait. Soon we'll have help for you; soon we'll be in Slobberram's Vale. Soon we'll get Slobberram to give you a ride."

Barny listened to the multifaceted sounds of her voice. Sometimes the liquid trilling of the blackbirds was interspersed by the shriller calls of the mockingbird. Then, at other times the melody of the nightingale cut through the doubts of his mind, leading him always onward.

An unusually shrill whistle startled him. He looked around to find the source of the noise. Out of the swirling vapours came a strange looking creature. A short-necked camel crossed with a fluffy kitten... no, a slobbering boxer crossed with a furry llama.

"This is Slobberram, he's agreed to give you a ride, haven't you big boy?"

Barny realised that he could understand most of the short, sharp series of whistles emitted by Slobberram. The benign beast even offered to keep his head down so that he wouldn't slobber all over Barny.

"Good boy, I knew you wouldn't want to offend our guest."

Slobberram crouched low, allowing Barny to mount. A short blast of whistles informed Barny that he had little to fear.

"Relax, all is easy on the back of Slobberram, sit back and enjoy the ride."

"Thank you Slobberram, you've made my life easier, my legs weren't keeping up with Earth Mother's fast pace."

"Never mind, no one can keep up with Earth Mother in the long run, she outlasts us all."

"Enough chatter you two - let's move, for the festival won't wait."

Earth Mother set off at pace. It seemed to Barny that even Slobberram was finding the going a little tough. Barny also realised the ride afforded him a few moments to look around and take in the landscape, or more precisely the lack of it. The swirling mists pervaded, clinging to the undergrowth and shrubbery with a stubborn tenacity.

"Why can't we see the sky? How will we see the moon rise if we cannot even see the treetops?"

"That's why we're making haste; we need to get above the swirling."

"Earth Mother, I still have so many questions, won't you please tell me what's going on?"

"Right, your persistence is finally getting the better of me. You may begin with your questions but only one at a time. If I feel like answering I will, otherwise you must wait the given period before

asking another."

Barny thought for a few minutes. He'd better choose his line of questioning carefully; he didn't want to cause Earth Mother more agitation. He thought he'd noticed, that when she became agitated, her eyes flashed more toward the lower end of the spectrum and her song became shriller. He didn't want to waste a question by asking how long the given period would be because he had a suspicion it could be anything from a few minutes to a few hours.

"Mother Earth, how did I get here?"

"You travelled with Gandalf and the Eagles. They were your guides."

"What! You must be joking with me. Gandalf is a fictional character created by Tolkien. How on earth could he have any part in this tale?"

Barny shut his mouth promptly when he noticed Earth Mother's eyes flashing red.

"Slowly now, you'll be upsetting the wizards."

"Sorry Earth Mother, this is just too farfetched for me to take in so easily. I loved Gandalf in the books and movies… he was a fictional hero of mine but for me to now suddenly believe that he had a part to play in transporting me here is rather rich."

"Hush child, he will smite you down for insubordination when he hears of this."

Icy chills crept up and down Barny's back, the hairs all over his body sprung up as if a strong static force had enveloped him. Suddenly he believed it all. Suddenly he knew his fate hung in the balance and that at any second his existence could be terminated by a mere thought by Earth Mother or her associates.

"Phew, I see it all. You and Gandalf are friends, you and Gandalf planned this trip for my benefit, didn't you?"

Earth Mother's eyes flashed a mixture of emerald green and violet which pleased Barny sufficiently to encourage his next question.

"But Earth Mother, where are we?

"We are in the nether forests of Axenopia, a vast expanse hidden from the evils of men and their machines by the swirls."

"Strange, I've never heard of Axenopia. Is it in Asia?"

"No child, we're very far away from Asia, in fact, we're very far away from the Earth you know. We're on a distant cousin of your planet. We're on the planet Westorinia in The Red Mists Galaxy."

Earth Mother paused, as if waiting for Barny's next question but he was so dumbfounded that he remained quiet. It would take him a while to digest what he'd heard. His confusion deepened but he felt at ease. As long as Earth Mother addressed him as *child,* he seemed on the right track, or so he thought.

"We'll soon reach the outskirts of the Rainbow Queen's realm. She's expecting us and will provide shelter for the night at one of her outstations. We can't be out after dark for evil lurks in the woods. Men have taken to prowling after dark, causing much trouble and disturbance."

"Are men here too?"

"Yes, men are everywhere; they've polluted many planets in many galaxies. They corrupt and destroy, that's why we of the Elder Councils have to keep the traditions to ward off the evils of men and their accomplices."

"So, are you and Gandalf friends?"

Barny was about to add a second question but fortunately realised his folly just in time. Patience child, *patience*, he chided himself.

"There was a time, when I lived more often in your world, then we saw much of each other but now we only meet once every 500 of your earth's years. In those times you could say we were friends, but then Merlin became jealous and the earth people became too greedy... so I made my way across here to stay."

"Wow... your tales are so incredible. Imagine being friends with Gandalf and Merlin all in one go. Who else did you know?"

"A few of the others... I once met Legolas... and that little fellow with the hairy feet. He was too silly for words so I didn't pay him much heed. Quiet now; rest that overactive tongue of yours for a while. I need to concentrate on the path ahead because we're coming to the edges of the Grey Marsh... an area of treacherous ground between Axenopia and the Rainbow Queen's haven."

Their pace slowed right down. Earth Mother stopped at one point to conjure up a staff so she could prod at the earth. Slobberram began snorting, just like an agitated horse, thought Barny.

"Calm down Slobber, you'll attract all sorts of nasties in our direction with your noise. Calm down, I'll not lead you into trouble."

The going slowed at each pace until Earth Mother found the link, the path she was searching for.

"Not a minute too soon, if we stay around here much longer the spiders will be crawling all over us. Not even Slobberram can fight through their webs. Let's get moving again, we need to get through the marsh rapidly for soon the twilight will put us in the betwixt or between. That will spell dread for the mission."

The darkness descended rather rapidly but Barny noticed the frequent low toned hooting sounds. It seemed to him as if Slobberram followed these sounds and soon his suspicions were confirmed. Earth Mother was no longer leading but instead she was following close behind.

Barny sank deeper into the ample warmth of Slobberram's comfortable back and dozed off.

He woke to a strangely ethereal chorus of chanting, owl-like moaning hoots and hollers. On top of this, the sound of a thousand skylarks and nightingales competed with robins, corncrakes and blackbirds and the sounds of flocks of other birds. Yet, there was no noise, it sounded like an orchestrated cacophony of the sweetest order. Heaven, thought Barny, must sound similar on a sunny day.

Fairy lights danced all around… beautiful shapes dancing, twirling about in the moonlight.

Moonlight? He realised he could see stars and moons. Two moons! They must have navigated the marshes and managed to get away from the swirling mists because all around he could see the countryside. Yes, it wasn't in daylight but even so, it looked enchanting. The sights were overwhelming, as if Earth Mother had morphed into multitudes of equally beautiful maidens of various shades and hues of the rainbow that were all gyrating about just for his pleasure… sensually enticing, drawing his gaze from one surreal pleasure to the next.

Where was he? He couldn't remember dismounting from Slobberram or for that matter, where was Slobberram? How had he arrived here? Why had he landed here… in this paradise of beauty?

"Earth Mother… Earth Mother…"

His voice trailed off, he realised a million Earth Mothers were all around, so who would answer? Who would know? Who would help him establish the meaning of it all? Who?

"Yes child, you were calling."

"Was I?"

He saw the flashing… cobalt blue changing and interspersed with flecks of turquoise. Then soft orangey mauve, not threatening, no… warm and inviting. Maybe she understood his confusion… his desire for… for what? Desire…

"Child, we've arrived at the Rainbow Queen's place. These are her aides, she's offered their help, and she knows our plight. The queen has laid on a restful evening's entertainment. You'll feast your senses, your dreams will be warm, your slumbers enriching."

Barny groaned, the sights and smells around asked for participation.

"I don't want sleep, I don't want dreams… I want to be part of the festivities… yes, I do!"

"Don't worry child, soon you will, soon you'll be the centre of attraction, soon you'll be the key to the ceremony. Soon!"

Barny thought he was drifting off but couldn't be sure. He opened one eye, just a slither. He tried to see what was going on around him but he sensed rather than saw the bright sunlight streaming into the clearing between the massive old trees.

His confusion deepened for he was certain he'd only seconds before been surrounded by thousands of beautiful beings all seeming to be the sole reason for his existence. Now here he was, opening his eyes to bright sunrise, lying flat on his back in the middle of a large clearing. Where were they all? What had happened to his dream? Dream? He thought Earth Mother had arranged the festivities but now he wondered if she'd deserted him here in the middle of the forest.

He sat up slowly. Why did he feel so totally dehydrated? Why did he feel a sense of foreboding? Why did he feel as though he'd been abandoned? What had happened to him? Not long ago he was flying fighter jets for the air force, now he thought he'd been skyjacked and thrown into a warped other dimension.

Should he shout out? Should he pick a direction and walk towards some point on some imaginary horizon? Why had Earth Mother abandoned him? Why was his reality so surreally unreal?

"Why, why… WHY?"

His scream echoed off the walls of lush vegetation, reverberating in the thin air. His scream also woke the forest. Suddenly the air was filled with the birdsong he'd heard the night before. Suddenly, out of nowhere, Slobberram was beside him.

"What? *Where did you come from?* How did you just materialise out of thin air? What's happening to me? Am I dreaming again?"

"Oh shut up Barny, stop being so dramatic. I was having a nap until you split the air with your hollers."

Barny stared at the drooling giant of a four-legged horse dog camel… whatever. Was this creature for real? Accusing him of being dramatic! Some ride he'd been dealt this time.

"Nap on then Slobber, I was just a bit dazed when I woke from my slumbers. I was sure that a few seconds ago I saw myself in a hospital bed, surrounded by sullen looking nurses. I was convinced they were shaking their heads in disbelief… I don't know why. But then I woke to find myself here in the meadow… alone."

Barny looked around again, his eyes fully adjusted to the bright sunshine.

"Where is everyone Slobber? Where is Earth Mother and all the

Rainbow Queen's assistants?"

"They're all resting… or preparing for the ceremony. Tonight is the great night, your night!"

"Why is it my night? Earth Mother kept saying I must be patient because soon it will be my night now you say it's tonight. What's going to happen tonight?"

"The two moons rise at precisely the same time, that's what! Then their trajectories cross… a perfect eclipse… only one moon in the sky! That is the moment of perfect harmony… of inception… of fertility. That is the moment when you'll be immortalised!"

A shrill screech rent the air…

"Enough Slobberram... enough!"

An electrifying chill overcame him… as if Earth Mother's harsh reprimand was cauterising Slobberram's words from his mind.

What now? What had the beast said to cause such dismay? He didn't know exactly what was happening but he realised there was no longer any sign of the Slobber. The faint ozone odour mingled with a wisp of cordite and hung in the air for a few seconds.

He looked around. Was he dreaming? Just moments earlier he could have sworn he'd seen Slobberram, now his senses messed with his mind. What was happening to him?

"Earth Mother… have I lost my mind? I'm sure I saw you chatting with a strange beast a few minutes ago. He was a funny looking creature… one I'd never set eyes on before. Funny, I feel funny…"

"Don't worry child, you were only having strange dreams but don't fear... Earth Mother will make it all better for you."

"Earth Mother… why am I here? I feel pain in my feet… my legs are on fire… my muscles hurt… what is happening to me? Am I going insane?"

"No child... you're just suffering the after effects of our long journey through the swirls and swamps. You're worn out by all last night's dancing and celebrations. Remember... all the Rainbow Queen's helpers?"

Barny listened intently yet he vaguely thought Earth Mother must've briefly touched his upper arm for he felt her powers shooting through his torso, down into his aching legs. Her calming tones lulled him into a tranquil doze.

Barny's slumber deepened. Soon he was dreaming of a mixture of pleasure and pain. He dreamed of the dancing forest of girls, all cavorting with him and with each other. Then, in flashes of blinding pain, he felt the flames licking at his feet and legs.

He dreamed of nurses… one asking the other if they thought the patient was comfortable. He heard the other say the morphine seemed to be helping. Fortunately, these parts of the dream were only brief snippets, more like momentary flashbacks to another era.

Barny wasn't sure if he was awake or still dreaming but the events were happening so quickly it didn't really matter. Earth Mother led him up the stairs of a large hexagonal stone platform and paraded him all along the perimeter. The throngs of helpers looked expectantly upwards. Their beauty could be seen from this distance, even in the low twilight.

Look at them all, he thought… nowhere was there a male to be seen. Here he was, their master, their superior being. They'd all come from far and wide to see him. He was their future… he brought fertility to the Rain Queen's realm. He was the answer… the future.

Barney failed to notice the large wood pile in the centre of the stone platform. He also failed to comprehend the purpose of the structure. He was so enthralled by the prospects of becoming the fertility god that they'd all been waiting for! Yes, he would be their future. He would be crowned during the rising of the two moons. He couldn't wait to go down and mingle with this expectant throng of beauty.

Little did Barny know that Earth Mother's trance was so strong that he would willingly climb onto the pyre when the time arrived. Little did he realise the outcome of the ceremony choreographed by Earth Mother and the elders!

A few minutes after arriving atop the stone platform Earth Mother stopped the parading and stood with Barny. They looked out over the sea of expectation towards the near horizon. An ethereal glow was creeping slowly upwards. Within minutes the crests of the two moons appeared above the forests.

"Look child, here come the moons… look there towards the right… that's Holy Man Moon… when he covers the Virgin Moon your moment will arise! Your fertility will mingle with those gathered below!"

Barny watched in awe. The slightly larger Man Moon rose from right to left while the brighter Virgin Moon was climbing into its path from the left. He stared, expecting the two moons to collide. Earth Mother knew his thoughts.

"No child, they will miss but we will have the perfect eclipse… you will witness something that only happens every 500 earth years. Enjoy the spectacle… enjoy the moment for it is truly yours…"

Earth Mother raised her arms and waved to the swirling masses below. The sounds of birdsong and scents rising upward became more intense. The fragrance of a million ripe blooms filled the heavy air. Barny understood in a flash that the scents were the inviting arousal aromas of the enchanted crowd. He sensed, more that saw, the perfection billowing upwards. They were ready.

He wanted to see more so he climbed onto the wood structure in the centre of the platform. He was totally caught up in the moment and raised his arms as well. He waved. The sounds and scents seemed to magnify tenfold. The light of the moons reflected off the radiant skins below. They glowed, yes, he was sure they were glowing in all the colours possibly imaginable to man.

He felt faint at the stunning sight. The moment overwhelmed him but just then he lifted his eyes to see the disc of the Virgin Moon slowly sliding behind the Man Moon. He was covering her! Soon his moment would arrive!

Earth Mother looked up at Barny. The moment was upon her. She felt a twinge of regret but knew she had to light the fires of fertility otherwise they would all wane away. She lifted one arm and pointed at the sky. She twirled and twisted. Her energy parted the heavens above and drew out the lightning bolt that lit the pile of wood, turning it into a funeral pyre.

Earth Mother watched the ecstasy surging through Barny's spent body. His eyes lit up like sapphires… his curling blond locks shone like gold in the spreading flames.

"Now my child, you must become one with the planet. Your energy will fly out towards those who are ready below. Not all will be lucky enough to be touched by you."

Earth Mother waited. Barny glanced down at her for a fleeting moment. His eyes shone with immense pride and love. Yes, thought she, he was the one. He was their future!

Still Earth Mother waited. She needed to hear the final signal before completing the fertility ceremony. She spoke softly, just loud enough for Barny to make out the faint sounds.

"Look child, see the moons become one. See their combined brightness illuminate the waiting masses. See, the Man Moon hasn't dimmed the Virgin's light... look, the two have united... their radiance is shining brighter than your sun."

Again, Earth Mother paused. A silence descended as she waited. The whole gathering waited for the final act to unfold. Then she heard the signal from the distant Earth,

"Sister, who is he? He's so very handsome, isn't he?"

"Yes nurse, he is too handsome to leave us now but I'm afraid the morphine won't keep him alive much longer."

Sister Bernadette glanced at the novice. She noticed the tears streaming down her pretty cheeks.

"Barny Strong, that's who you see, he's a fighter pilot. The firemen pulled him from the burning cockpit only minutes before the plane exploded. He'd managed to land his badly shot up jet just before it burst into flames."

Earth Mother listened in silence, waiting for the moment. Then she heard it.

"Pity life is so fragile nurse, it's over now. He's gone!"

At that exact moment Earth Mother's shriek tore through the night. The eclipse was complete as the fire roared all around Barny. Earth Mother began slowly turning on her own axis, very slowly at first but soon she stirred up a gentle tornado. The breeze swirled around the pyre, drawing sparks and embers away, yet the blaze intensified.

Earth Mother felt the quickening of the flames rushing through her. Life, yes… his fire was searing through her being. Her spinning intensified, spreading the sparks and embers of life wider and wider until the billowing smoke clouds obscured the two moons, blotting out their glow. The choking cloud enveloped the gathering, providing momentary solitude for each of the masses, allowing everyone their brief moment of private, hot climax.

Only when the altar's fire expended its energy of life did Earth Mother stop spinning. The ritual was over - she knew the scorched smell of flesh would again rejuvenate those gathered below. She also knew the blast she'd received would strengthen her powers even more. She knew… soon she'd be able to return to Earth to reclaim her rightful throne and be with her fighter pilot.

Dublin Streets – Meeting Oscar Wilde

Ralph's famously familiar words ring through my mind as I walk out of Connolly Station. Only difference, I tweak the key line slightly.

"Let me take you by the hand and lead you through the streets of Dublin..."

My figurative journey began after reading a blog post by an author about metafiction. The piece sparked an idea. Dublin's streets are so full of literary genius memories that it would be a treat to walk where the greats had once set foot.

I'd very quickly made up my mind that I wasn't going to do a Leopold Bloom on myself. The great Joyce had taken all of 260 000 words to do that so where on earth would I find the inner strength to do even one of the eighteen episodes? Anyway, I wanted to interview a few of the greats, I didn't want to interview their creations. Or, did I?

Then another thought dawned. Did Joyce not first do short stories? The Dubliners? Maybe I should walk where The Dubliners lived and walked. Too many characters and places. I was confusing myself in the process. Maybe I should walk back up the stairs to the station, get on a train and head home to review my plans.

I didn't. I keep walking in the direction of the Liffey, reminded of the graffiti on one of the buildings along the North Quays.

The Liffey cuts The City like a meandering blue vein...

Author unknown, artist unknown but a simple city truism none-the-less. The river cuts through the city like so many other rivers cleave cities asunder. Here, I'm reminded, it separates the learned rich from the unwashed poor. Well, that's how the South-siders would make it out to be.

I catch myself humming... *let me take you by the hand...* yes, let me do just that as I head across the Samuel Beckett Bridge in the direction of the Grand Canal Basin. I pause for a moment or seven. I pause to look down toward the port area. There's a ferry making its early morning departure. A massive steel structure, once rumoured to be the largest car ferry in the world, aptly named Ulysses. A bridge and a boat linking two famous sons of the city.

Get a move on, I mutter to myself. I scold myself to get going because I could stand on the bridge for half of forever. I love the atmosphere, all the young ones going by. The river's flow hurries along, water sucked all the way from Kildare by the fast receding tide. Seagulls screech defiantly overhead, to remind the humans below that the place still belongs to Mother Nature.

I reluctantly walk away. There's a mission to pursue and as hard as I may, I have to get moving in the direction of Merrion Square. I glance at my watch. Yes, I'll make it with a few minutes to spare.

As I walk along Pearce Street, I make a mental note to research his contribution to Irish literature. I have words with myself, again. Was he a political leader or a writer? Both? Flip, it's not always easy for a foreigner to know all the smaller details. Never mind, now concentrate on the meeting you're heading for. Get Beckett, Pearce and Joyce out of your head for a few hours.

I swing a left, up Westland Row, past the station and the church and keep going. The strident introduction to Tchaikovsky's 1812 Overture greets me as I approach the Royal Irish Academy of Music. The sound is interrupted as an off-key violin attempts to join. Just as well, the discord would put a mating tomcat's howls out of business.

I round the corner as the traffic noise overtakes the restart of 1812. Enough Tchaikovsky for one day, thank you. Not far now to the meeting point. I head into Merrion Square after passing the house where Wilde was born. I have to wait a minute or two for a group of tourists to complete their photo session with Oscar. It allows me a few moments to prepare. I set up the camping chair I'd lugged along. I fish in the backpack and retrieve my notepad.

I watch the last of the tourists wander away. Now is my moment, now is that point in time where I put all my gut feel in motion. I look up at the reclining figure of the great man and pluck up the courage to dive into the interview.

"Be yourself; everyone else is already taken." [1]

"Cute, very cute, beginning your session with my words."

"Quotation is a serviceable substitute for wit." [2]

"Now you're overdoing it... throwing my words at me, as if you've taken my sword from me and using it as your weapon."

"Please accept my apology Sir, I had to get your attention one way or another. You'll have to agree though, those words of yours have merit."

I sit, gathering my thoughts. It's no easy task interviewing a great, especially a sharp wit like Oscar Wilde. I have to tread carefully. I glance at my notes once more, more as a way of gathering my thoughts than anything else. I know what my line of questions will be. All I now need to do is find the correct tone and pace of proceeding.

"Sir, may I begin by asking if I may ask a few questions? Two themes really, relating to your relationships with fellow Dubliners."

"You may indeed but not before you promise to call me by my name. Oscar will do just fine, thank you."

"Thank you Sir, er… pardon, thank you Oscar."

I pause, thoughts racing. I toy with the idea of changing my questions even before I've asked the first. No, stick to your preparation, or the whole process may flop.

"OK, let me begin by asking if you may have written a better version of Dracula if Florence Balcombe had chosen you over Bram Stoker?"

I glance in his direction. His expression remains emotionless, as if he's mildly irritated that I should be cocky enough to speak of his early flame.

"Let me answer you thus… *in this world there are only two tragedies. One is not getting what one wants, and the other is getting it." [3]*

I'm taken aback. He'd grabbed his sword and deflected the sting right back at me. A faint shiver of dread creeps into my consciousness. Did I really think I could spar with this genius and come away in one piece?

"If I'd got what I'd wanted, do you think I would have become the man I did? Do you think domestication would have suited me that early in life? Or, may you be suggesting that it was dear Florence's impact on Bram's life that drove him to create the dark fantasy?"

The pause hung heavy in the chilly autumn air. I'm sure he purposely let the words linger, purposely allowing time for the ideas to sink in.

"An idea that is not dangerous is unworthy of being called an idea at all." [4]

He's at it again, throwing his words at me… thrust and parry… verbal sparring. Is he encouraging me to keep going or is he leading the interview and not me? Maybe, I thought, it would be safer for me to beat a retreat now.

"The final word on dear Florence - *Between men and women there is no friendship possible. There is passion, enmity, worship, love, but no friendship.* [5] She wanted friendship… I wanted passion and the pleasure of her beauty."

I'm not sure I'm entirely happy with his answers but I think better of it not to be pressing him to elaborate. Instead, I plough on with the next question.

"Would you and Francis Bacon have hit it off if your paths crossed? I mean, you were known for your flamboyance and he was often tagged as a bon vivant."

"The only artists I have ever known who are personally delightful are bad artists. Good artists exist simply in what they make, and

consequently are perfectly uninteresting in what they are." [6]

"Do I understand you correctly, are you saying he was a bad artist? I'm not sure…"

I pause, not sure how best to proceed. I get the feeling he's leading me into a trap. Worse still, a trap of my own making.

"Art is the most intense mode of individualism that the world has known· [7] We both had our art to pursue. We didn't need each other, for friendship or as crutches. Just think of it like this, separately we retained the enigma of *what ifs*, together we may have bored the world."

I remain silent, again allowing his words to wash over me. I need time to assimilate the wisdom. How much time, I ask myself? A day, a week… a lifetime?

"Let me continue my line of thought. You know some critics branded me a mediocre poet, this is what I have to say to doubters - *A great poet, a really great poet, is the most unpoetical of all creatures. But inferior poets are absolutely fascinating. The worse their rhymes are, the more picturesque they look. The mere fact of having published a book of second-rate sonnets makes a man quite irresistible. He lives the poetry that he cannot write. The others write the poetry that they dare not realise." [8]*

I'm sure he noticed my discomfort and took pity on me. I'm convinced he'd allowed me time to answer my own questions, if only I would open my eyes. To that effect I took his final words to heart. I pack my things, thank him and depart with his wisdom ringing in my ears.

"The aim of life is self-development. To realise one's nature perfectly - that is what each of us is here for." [9]

[1,2,3,4,5,6,7,8,9] All italics are OW quotes taken from GoodReads dot com

The House Sitter

"You ever heard of Sitters United?"

A strange question, it seemed at the time. Especially strange when you'd only met the man a few minutes earlier. However, it's not as if he wasn't familiar looking. I'd seen him on at least three previous showings. He always hovered in the background, usually appearing engrossed in one of the landscapes on display.

I kept a wary eye on folk who seemed to hang back. You never knew when someone was going to attempt making off with one of your pieces. Landscapes, yes, that's what he's looking at. Yes, I convinced myself that he must be looking for something specific before he would approach to ask.

"Would you consider taking on a commission?"

Bloody hell, this could turn interesting. Some line of enquiry this fellow's pursuing. I looked him up and down. More for effect than anything else. He seemed respectable, upper middle class? No… his well-structured speaking tone suggested lower upper class.

My gaze lingered. How do I answer the man? He seemed impatient for a reply. His look hardened, the twinkle in the eye replaced by a steely glare.

"Have I startled you?"

"No, you haven't startled me. Rather caught me off guard because I'm not quite sure what you're really after."

"Ah good, you've found your tongue."

I watched a few seconds longer. Should I turn and walk away or entertain his questions? I'd allow him a few more seconds before making up my mind.

"Let me introduce myself. My name is Taigh McKenna."

This time I accepted his firm hand, the momentary grasp conveyed sufficient strength to place me on alert. He wouldn't take no for an answer lightly. His quizzical look dragged me back to the now.

"Pardon my rudeness but I do suggest you already know who I am."

"Yes Guy, I'm familiar with your identity. You may say I've spent the last few weeks getting to know you through your work."

"OK, you know who I am for sure. I've seen you stalking me for a few weeks. Why did you not introduce yourself earlier? I'm about to pack away my exhibit. Time to go, I'm afraid."

"Simple actually. I waited because I'd like to suggest we get a coffee as soon as you've stowed your wares."

The cheek of him, I thought, not only is he laying claim to my time, he's calling my paintings *wares*. Should I humour him or tell him where to shove his compliments?

"Make up your mind man, surely it can't be that difficult to have a cup of coffee with someone who's buying."

Statement… not request. Yes, he was used to having his own way. Probably middle upper-class, used to dictating terms to the lesser mortals.

"I'd be delighted to. Give me a few moments to dispose of my wares and I'll be all yours."

Fek him, I thought. Who is he to pitch up on a Saturday afternoon and shout the odds? I took my time. I even went over to Margaret who shows next to me to enquire after her partner's health.

"You ok, he's not harassing you, is he?"

Her hushed tones and worried look suggested that she'd copped on.

"No, thanks for asking. I'm trying to stall him a little. He's invited me for coffee and I'm sure he's after something other than a painting, but I don't know what."

"Well, maybe there's nothing sinister about his invite, you're just being over cautious, again."

"You think?"

Yes, her firm nod suggested that that's exactly what she thought.

"Get a move on, you're really pissing him off now."

"Great… that's just what I want to do. To show him I'm not his servant."

I turned and walked to the rear of my van. I checked that all the canvasses were correctly stowed before closing the doors.

"I'll have to move the van. Shall I meet you back here in a few minutes?"

His suspicious glance confirmed my thoughts.

"No, I won't do a runner. What would that help, you know where to find me, don't you?"

His smile did wonders for him, he shed years by not scowling.

"Regale Margaret, I'm sure she'll fill you in with a few saucy details."

I winked at him, my best know-it-all, come-hither wink. I didn't bother to wait for a response. I jumped into the van a drove around the corner. I was lucky to find free parking almost immediately. Good, that would allow me a few minutes to do an internet search. LinkedIn was quick to provide me with a brief profile.

Taigh McKenna, president and CEO of TMcK Holdings. Property, media, green energy investor. Director and board member of about 15 charity and arts organisations. All round good guy and highbrowed snob, thought I. Ok, let's go hear what Lord He-Haw wants of me.

I didn't have long to find out it seemed, friend Taigh was waiting at the corner.

"Come, follow me. Off we go, down the road to a little bistro down the next lane."

He gestured, outstretched arm, finger pointing. He'd put Napoleon to shame, I'm sure he would.

"Beats me though, how any eatery outside Paris could get away by using bistro in their name. Criminal misrepresentation, I tell you."

I had to hasten my step, he was in full flight… to the battlefield and beyond. He kept muttering, not in the slightest interested if I may like to venture a view or opinion. It was going to be a difficult evening, I surmised.

"Their saving grace? The food is good, the wine great and the cognac magnificent. Yes, they have their merits, despite claiming to be French."

It seemed he'd planned his running commentary to end at the exact moment when he opened the door to the restaurant. Nifty, effective way of impressing his guests.

"Good evening Sir, the usual spot?"

The pretty maître d's beaming smile suggested genuine affection and a welcoming warmth.

"Yes please Mary… the usual spot please and if anyone asks, I'm not in."

"That's fine, I'll send Robert in your direction in a minute or two."

Taigh continues to an isolated booth at the rear of the room. We enter, he closes the curtains and we make ourselves comfortable.

"You enjoy a good steak? If you do I recommend you give theirs a go. The reds are a great match so I usually have something light for a starter and get a full slab of meat to keep me busy for a while."

"I wasn't really planning on eating, I thought you'd invited me for a coffee?"

"Patience isn't one of your strengths, I suspect. All in good time, you'll have your coffee when your belly has been filled. I'll take the liberty of ordering on your behalf, they know my tastes so you can be assured of your enjoyment."

No use objecting, I thought. Just relax and enjoy, I told myself. Your lordship will do the thinking for you, all you need to do is act subservient.

We were soon savouring a great Bordeaux merlot along with

really well prepared steaks. The fries and veggies supplemented the meal perfectly. We enjoyed the meal in relative silence. However, it didn't take Taigh long to get going once the dirty plates disappeared.

"You're a very good artist. Why then would you be displaying your works at the Merrion Square weekend exhibits? Aren't those exhibits meant for up and coming wannabe's?"

"Firstly, thanks for the compliment. Secondly, I enjoy the fun of the open-air exhibits. Also, it exposes my work to many potential buyers who wouldn't necessarily go to galleries."

"Surely you have enough exposure during your official hangings? Pardon me if I wrong but my research suggests you often sell out way before the end of exhibits."

"Aha… not only have you taken me captive but you've researched my sales. Next you will inform me what my net worth may be."

"That I could do but I'm sure you'll think me bad mannered, if I do."

Again the smile softened his features. Yes, he was toying with me but in a harmless way, I hoped. I continued.

"The main reason why I'm out there every second weekend is to get rid of as many of my lesser works as I can. I often have trial or experimental canvasses. I used to toss them in the skip until an ex of mine suggested I finish them off and flog them. That was the best advice I ever got from any girl I've had the privilege of meeting."

He gave me a long hard look before ordering another round of drinks. I half raised my hand in protest, acutely aware that I was already well over the driving limit.

"Don't worry, I've arranged for a driver to take your van to a safe storage lock-up for the evening, he'll soon be here so would you please hand me the key?"

"Now you have me totally at your mercy, I have nowhere to run."

"Why would you want to run? Things may just be getting better for you."

He must've heard my suppressed sigh. The smile disappeared and his tone hardened when he spoke again.

"Ok, enough chit-chat. You must by now be burning to know what's really going on."

He glanced at me, our gaze locked for a few seconds. He lifted his glass in slow motion. Was he raising the glass in a toast or mock salute? I wouldn't know and neither would I ask. Let him speak, let me listen.

"Back to your art. You're good, your pieces fetch good money and are hung in private and public collections. I need your skills. As far as I can ascertain you're single, correct?"

“Yep. I’m single. The pressures of restrictive ties don’t go well with me. Anyway, I work better when I’m allowed my own space.”

“Grand, that means I’m potentially onto a winner. You see, I want you to take on a challenge for me. I’m suggesting you join Sitters United. I need you to build up a portfolio of house sits. That’s if you’re interested.”

I wouldn’t at that exact point have said I was interested, curious and at a loss maybe but not interested. Baffled, or was that too strong?

I’d never fancied brandy so the cognac wasn’t going down too well. I twirled the amber liquid around in the snifter, wondering how to proceed.

“Should I rather get you a whiskey?”

Bloody mind reader. I nodded, still not sure of a suitable answer. I held my tongue until the fresh drink arrived.

“I’m afraid I can’t see a reason for taking on your challenge… yet. But I’m sure it’s no issue because you’ll soon reveal the real reason why you want me to take up this new hobby.”

“Indeed. I want you to go into a few select residences. I’ve been working on a plan and it will entail you making accurate copies of artworks in these homes. That, in essence, is the crux of the challenge.”

I recall that I just sat and stared at him. Was he daft? Did he really think people would let me into their houses and allow me to make copies of their wall decorations? I shook my slowly, in disbelief.

“Look, you’re obviously used to getting what you want but in this case you may be pushing your luck too far. Why on earth would you plan on doing what you have in mind?”

I took a moment’s breather but before he replied I held up my hand in protest and continued.

“Has it dawned on you that your ideas may be criminal… or just plain immoral?”

“Yes… and no.”

“What? Now you’ve totally lost me. Mind you, I think that’s where I’d like to stay… totally lost and removed from your ideas.”

I slumped back into the chair. I stared at him over the rim of the tumbler while occasionally taking small sips. My expression must have been sufficiently stern as he waited a good few minutes before speaking again. I’d said all I felt necessary and couldn’t be bothered to open my mouth again other than to sip at the whiskey.

I wondered if he’d get me another when I placed the empty glass on the table. Maybe he’d expect me to pay for my dinner. Maybe that was a good idea. No favours taken. I was about to suggest that our meeting was over when he called for more whiskey. A bottle, ice and two fresh glasses. How mistaken I was, he wasn't planning on letting me off the hook without a full-blown assault.

"Right, let me explain a little better. I have three houses on the immediate list. I have squared the whole plan with the owners of these places. They are fully in on the proposed action."

My mind raced, so? Did that change matters much? Making fraudulent copies of paintings was never a good idea. I pondered and to his credit he didn't continue until he assumed I'd thought things through. This became the pattern each time he explained further. He'd pause, I'd sip and think and when he thought he'd allowed enough time he'd continue.

"I have letters of approval from each of the three. The letters state that you are welcome to house sit and more importantly, you are cleared to make copies of named paintings in each collection."

All good and well, how, at this moment in time, do I stop myself from getting totally inebriated? I reached for the water jug and filled my glass to the brim. Dublin tap water will have to do for a while.

"We plan to exhibit the originals at some point in the future but we don't want gaping holes in our collections."

"I notice you say we. That makes four of you in on the act, am I correct?"

"Yes, we're each contributing three works. In that way we'll gauge what our overall collections are worth."

"Would it not make better sense for Christie's or Sotheby's to value the works?"

"Yes and no."

Ah fek, here we go again. Punch and counterpunch. How long is he going to keep this up?

"Look, the way we see it is, if we hold an anonymous public showing of the works then representatives from anywhere could vie for the right to buy the collection. We're hoping that someone will want a particular work sufficiently to take the whole lot, thereby inflating the prices of the lesser works."

I had to admit, he may be onto something. Ok, here's my chance for a piece of the action.

"If I'm correct then you plan to show twelve pieces. Why don't I throw one of mine in… make it a lucky thirteen?"

"Yes, you may do just that. Now you've added the title for the show. *The Lucky Thirteen…* it has a good ring and implies that the collection is not to be broken up. Good one!"

Gosh, he was almost animated. For a change he took something from me and showed appreciation. Maybe the whole thing has merit after all? Maybe.

***

We met on a few more occasions in the weeks that followed and before I knew it I was working on copies of three of his originals. Two Americans, a Thomas Cole and a Kensett as well a lesser known 20th century Canadian. He offered a set fee for each piece which was great because I could work on my own stuff along with working on the copies.

Once he was satisfied that the works were accurate enough he took them away. I'd made sure to place a unique mark on each canvas. It wasn't easy but I found a way to add my initials in dot form within folds of clothing or hidden in landscape features. I photographed each of these marks for posterity. If ever one of my copies was put up for sale as an original I would be able to prove it was a copy.

At some point Taigh asked if I'd joined Sitters United yet. I couldn't see the reason but he insisted that I do. I wasn't sure how it would impact on my profile so he suggested I use a pseudonym.

Guy van Rhyn. It had a rather interesting ring to it. It sounded so arty that I began signing some of my painting with the name.

It wasn't long before I had my first glowing endorsement on the Sitters Unite website. Of course it was submitted by Taigh. He even mentioned my love and appreciation for the fine arts. This, he assured me, would ensure that folk knew I'd look after their precious works of art. Yes, I said… I'd know which the best are to steal. He dismissed my frivolity with a question.

"How would you fancy eight weeks in Southern France?"

"Who wouldn't fancy Southern France at this time of the year?"

"Well, it's time you have a look at Sitters… there's a couple advertising their place, they're looking for a single, non-smoker to look after their place while they're on their cruise. Get cracking man… they're just waiting for you to apply."

Taigh was doing all the background work and wasn't too impressed that I hadn't kept an eye on the website but then, to my defence, since when was I a house sitter?

"Will two months allow enough time to do three copies?"

"Depends on the size and complexity of the paintings. Anyhow, if I'm not done, I could always keep working on the pieces when I get back to Dublin."

"The one is a small painting attributed to Vermeer, girl with wineglass or something. The other is a Cezanne and the last an early 20th century French artist whose name slips my memory. We're back to the two well-known and one obscure theory."

We're also back to dragging me further into the fraudulent abyss.

By early in the New Year I'd completed the task and garnered another glowing appraisal on the Sitters site. Seemingly I was now an old hand. All I needed was a third five-star review and I'd be classed a master.

Taigh was happy, he was halfway to the target and I didn't have to wait long before my next assignment. A mail arrived in the inbox from an interested Spanish contact. Would I like to look after their villa on the Galician coast? Spring in Spain? You bet I'd like that.

I sent Taigh a text. Should I accept the invitation? He called almost immediately.

"Yes… you're going to enjoy this one. There's a very early Dali self-portrait that is a must. Also, a Goya and the lesser known one is 20th century Mexican impressionist piece, by Gonzalez. You have the whole of April and May to get this assignment out of the way."

Mr Guy van Rhyn was a busy boy. Paintings here and paintings there. Somehow, I had to find time to keep my regulars happy as well. I managed to persuade two galleries to include my work in group showings. Another happily accepted my suggestion that we show much later in the next year. Yes, they actually wanted a different drawcard before Christmas so that would work out perfectly.

I kept all of them happy by saying I'd be travelling so they could expect a change of scenery and maybe even style. I'd long wanted to do stark, barren landscapes. Broody, ethereal kind of stuff. Contrasting primary colours… ideas thrown into the blender in my mind and splattered out on canvas. Would it work? Who knows? Who cares?

Spain in the spring. Real seafood, ham, chorizo and so many other delights. I had difficulty getting the three pieces done and needless to say, I hardly worked on anything of my own. The spring went by rather rapidly and before I could say Rioja, I was packing my bags.

I was hardly back in Dublin when the phone rang. My impatient master was already asking when I'd like to go off to the Netherlands. Autumn poplars along canal banks? Late autumn I suggested. I needed time to get my paintings completed for the group exhibitions I'd be a part of.

"Will you be down at the Merrion Square this weekend? Fine, I'll meet you around five on Saturday afternoon. Why? Because I want to see what you've been up to lately."

When I noticed him, he seemed engrossed in one of my latest Spanish landscapes. I left him be and carried on chatting with American tourists who wanted to take home three or four works. Would I ship?

Would buying in bulk get them a better price? All good for the bank balance.

We arranged to meet in the week so I could show them a few more works but before they walked off, they'd paid a deposit and reserved two Irish landscapes. I began packing up and was about to fetch the van when Taigh approached.

"I'll have that Spanish mountain-scape please, if I may? I'll throw dinner in on top of the asking price."

I smiled at him before muttering my delight.

"Today is truly a great day. I've just sold three pieces in the last five minutes and now I've even solicited a feed. And to think, I was going to offer paying for your dinner."

The evening went by in a blur. Yes, Taigh and his associates were all delighted with my reproductions. Now we needed to get the last three completed so that they could arrange their exhibition. Taigh wanted to target the Far East. Maybe even China but more likely Hong Kong.

Then he filled me in on a small detail that I'd never even considered.

"None of the partners know of our plans. This is a project between the four… well, with you included, the five of us. We are in the throes of setting up an offshore venture capital consultancy. Private, and I mean private."

I sat back taking it all in. Firstly, it seems I'll now be a partner in something I'd never dreamed of being involved in. Secondly, were the four of them hiding this from their partners for a reason? I bet. This whole affair was turning into a monumental tax dodge as well as cutting net worth from their estates without anyone but the five of us knowing.

"You're far too cute for your own good."

That was the only response I could dredge up. These latest developments had me totally cornered. I'd already delivered nine copies, forgeries, facsimiles… whatever you want to call them, the art establishment and Interpol would look on me as a total swindle, should the truth be known.

"You've got me by the short and curlies. Haven't you?"

Taigh's face softened, his charming smile seemed capable of defusing a nuclear standoff.

"I think you may just be a little over imaginative. Are you suggesting we're doing something we shouldn't?"

"Yes, I am. You're planning to substitute real masterpieces with copies. How on earth will the unsuspecting public know if you switch the paintings after they've paid for them?"

"Never, because we'll only sell the originals."

"Ok, say three years down the line one of the partners decides to put a piece up for auction. What then? Even worse, say you do switch all twelve pieces and when the original goes up for auction then the whole scam is uncovered."

I realised I may have gone just a step too far. His look suggested I'm on the verge of being murdered. Seems I may have had a go at his integrity, or at the least that's how he interpreted my take on things.

"Guy, do you really think we're going to compromise our reputations… and yours, with an ill-conceived scam? Really, I didn't expect such a negative comment from you. After all, it's not as if you've signed any of the works in your own name."

I remained quiet, regurgitating his words. Ok, he has a point but these days forensic labs can establish much about any artwork. Still, I would have to reserve my doubts. No good antagonising Taigh any further. I tried to undo some of the damage with a lame question.

"I wonder, for the Lucky Thirteen expo, should I make a copy of my original as well?"

"You could just as well, using your pseudonym. No, that wouldn't work, if one of the partners noticed your name in the future, they may link you to the Sitters United stay in their houses."

More messy details, thought I. The quagmire deepens… the mud getting stickier by the minute and my nightmare scream running scene getting darkly sinister. Imagine if something goes wrong after the Lucky Thirteen exhibit. Well, at least I have the consolation that I'd be a continent or two away from the immediate action.

***

The Netherlands was a roaring success. Cheese, chocolate and gallons of great beer. I even toyed with the idea of experimenting with some of the Amsterdam coffee shop wares. I missed the great outdoor flower fields but the autumn colours along the canals added their own charm to the paintings I worked on.

As for the three copies, it turned out to be less simple than I hoped for as replicating an early Mondrian had its difficulties. He seemed to have used inferior paint and it showed. The cracking took a considerable amount of trial and error to perfect. In the end, I stressed the canvas by rolling and folding it up a few times. Then I had the brainwave of leaving it in a warm oven for a few minutes.

The first few attempts didn't work too well so I tried spraying a fine coating of fixer on the drying surface before placing the canvas in the oven. The results were more than promising so I continued working on four separate canvasses, applying more or less fixer at different stages of the paint application. In and out of the oven went the paintings until the results were just as I hoped.

By the time I'd completed the Mondrian and selected the best ones to keep I was left with a small pile of canvasses to dispose of. Most of the experimental pieces were ripped as fine as I could before I took their remains for long walks. The trash bins all over the Apeldoorn area all became unwilling recipients of my messed Mondrian's. I hoped the bins' contents went to an incinerator.

The other two works were less taxing. Both were by South African artists I'd never heard of. A Pierneef landscape along with a Bosch floral arrangement. Artists not known to me but the more I learned about them the more I appreciated their work.

The Netherlands assignment ended far too quickly. Actually, all of them had. I retained the one Mondrian copy, someday I may be brave enough to hang it in my house. Taigh took possession of the three copies. He was as happy as a schoolboy on a rollercoaster. Soon, he promised, I'd have my share of the rewards. He reminded me to drop in one of my paintings which I did later in the week.

Months later Taigh passed on the good news. The Lucky Thirteen exhibition sale went off way better than expected. Taigh confirmed that one unidentified buyer had taken the whole collection and as it contained a fair share of masters the person hadn't even quibbled over the collective price. Did I want my 7.5% share now or did I want the proceeds to be invested in the holding company?

***

That was five years ago. Since then I'd stayed busy with my house sitting activities. I'd become quite a popular sitter but mostly, I really enjoyed the travel and opportunity of living the life of a local in any given location. On occasion I even turned down requests because of diary clashes.

I met Taigh maybe twice a year and only did on average three copies in any given year. He would let me know what he wanted copied and I'd oblige. On the balance of things this was the way I preferred it, I could concentrate on my likes and dislikes wherever I stayed.

Then, about 18 months ago came the big one. Taigh scheduled a meeting and ran the details past me. He'd put this whole thing together as long as five years in advance, just for this assignment. I'd be looking after a rather unassuming four bed house in the Algarve. Nothing strange there until he informed me about the very robust security system.

Then he rammed the missile home. It was the house of his ex-wife. The place contained at least 20 originals. As he put it, all fleeced off him during the divorce settlement. I would have a full eight months to do my deeds. All I needed to do was confirm my availability on the website before his ex-wife selected another sitter.

I wondered, aloud, how he'd managed to convince his ex to select me as the sitter.

"Aha… I didn't. She'd been planning this year long extreme adventure trip for many years. She enquired from others about what to do with the house while away and one of my distant acquaintances suggested she have a look at your portfolio at Sitters Unite."

He went on to explain that the happy lady was quite a few years younger than him and at some point, had become bored with the upper crust easy life. So, she'd made off with a much younger man. Not that he minded, well, apart from his paintings, he was quite happy for her to set off on her own so he could continue with his side-line activities without her finding out. Imagine, he said, if she'd found out he was sporadically seeing three different women on the continent.

Oh well, some boys have it all, don't they?

"I should take you along on a visit to Lake Garda. The delectable Florentine has a very attractive twin sister. Maybe you could do a few *nude* works."

That smile of his. It lit the room, reminding me of the time we'd first met and I'd thought him mad to suggest the scheme I've been part of for more than five years.

"So, pack your sunscreen and beach gear. The house is about 100 meters from one of the best beaches in the Western Algarve. Little village of Alvor."

Taigh paused to let the words sink in, he winked sheepishly before continuing.

"You'll find many pine-topped cliff seascapes all within a kilometre of the house. However, I've got a list of 15 for you to get done for me. This time, we're going to replace the originals with your copies before you complete your stay."

No, I wasn't even going to bother expending a single breath in protest. He knew what he wanted and knew I'd oblige. I mean, who was ever going to uncover our switch. Amazing, I thought. Now I'm believing my own bull, all the doubts of the past seemed to have drifted away. Or had they? I'd be lying if I said I could put my finger on the feeling of ill gnawing at me.

That was then. This is now. Here I sit, shifting from one buttcheek to the other, trying to alleviate the numbing pain in my posterior. The realisation of my current situation rapidly expelling the memories of the good times. Mistakes. Small mistakes.

Like believing we will get away with the heist and never be held accountable. All went well, until Taigh's ex-wife's partner went and croaked. Not only did his heart give out on him totally unexpected but he was lucky enough to be in the act when it happened.

A tiny detail Taigh had forgotten to share with me… his ex-wife's partner just so happened to be his youngest sibling. Apparently, the ex was so traumatised by the whole thing that she fled and within days had wanted to be rid of the whole bang-shute in the Algarve.

Next mistake? Taigh had reacted too slowly to the news of the sale and when he attempted to buy back the art in the house, he was informed that an unnamed auctioneer had the paintings under lock and key.

Good, we all thought, until the news filtered through that the unidentified auctioneer wanted to establish the providence of a few of the works because he was under the impression that a few of the pieces had been sold on the open market only a few months ago.

Mistake!

I'd got the jitters and booked a flight to South America. Columbia's wild landscapes had always been on my agenda and seeing as the country had non-existent extradition treaties with almost the whole world, I felt safe.

Another mistake. Massive mistake.

It seems one of the patrons most burned by the sale of the stolen heist had been an influential drug lord from you guessed where. Apparently, my name was leaked to this gentleman… apparently in exchange for him dropping the case with the authorities. Seemingly a secret deal had been made with him… he could retain his ill-gotten gains.

So… after all the years of being part of the scheme I was to be exhibited as the sacrificial lamb. Little consolation I'd get by the prospect of the impending 20-year house sit… in one of the world's most feared prisons! I wonder if they'd throw in art supplies.

The Old Man and the Fish

The bony old finger slowly followed the line of words across the page. The sun-stained skin brown against the pale white of the page. Knotty knuckles cast strange shadows across the words while the calcified fingernail left a faint scratch beneath the words.

Manuel sat flat on the hard red earth, propped up against the trunk of a gnarled old olive tree beside his little cottage. Man and tree seemed joined, in life and antiquity. The dappled shade of the vines entangling the tree cast blurred shadows on the earth. The gentle sea breeze tugged at the leaves, changing the patterns on the ground. The breeze also tugged at the old man's tufty beard.

Manuel lifted his gaze away from the book. He sighed, a long, slow release of lonely emotion. He stared longingly at the blue ocean in the distance. How he longed to return to the waters, one last time. Maybe, he thought, the waters would welcome him with their chilly embrace. Maybe it was his destiny.

He rose slowly, his backside sore from sitting prone on the hard earth. His back ached, many years of hard toil leaving their toll on his old frame. He recalled days when he would sit for hours in that spot. He loved feeling the bark against his back and the direct contact with the earth. He loved gazing out at the ocean. Then he was young. Then he longed to go to sea with the men. He longed to prove himself out on the water. He longed to be counted as a man among the men of the village.

Now he was old. Now he was the second oldest inhabitant in the village. Yet he still longed for the ocean even though he'd long stopped going to sea. He didn't need to fish for a living anymore. His simple lifestyle's needs were well catered for by his only son. The son he'd helped educate, the son who'd gone off to the city to make it big.

The only son who sent money but never returned to the village. The son who'd forgotten his roots, the past he was ashamed of. Manuel recalled his one and only trip to the city. His son wanted to show him the bright lights but Manuel couldn't come to terms with the claustrophobia he suffered in the place. Madrid was too far away from the ocean.

Everything choked him. They made him get into tiny windowless boxes that took him many floors up. Then he had to look down at the ant-like people in the streets below. He didn't like the experience for it made him feel as if he was trying to play God.

Tomás, his son, had been so insistent in proving his wealth and status that he'd taken an apartment on the very top floor of Torre de Madrid. Manuel shivered slightly as he cast his mind back to that visit.

Twelve years later and he'd not seen his son. They'd parted at the station, the dapper young corporate whizz kid briefly shaking hands with the sunburnt old man. Even their clothes were worlds apart. The old man dressed in faded denims and check shirt, the younger son resplendent in his cut perfect Savile Row suit.

Worlds apart, yes, thought the old man. They lived in different time zones, their only link the Euros sent each month. Manuel sighed again. He shuffled toward the rear of the cottage to find a canvas chair in the lean-to shelter that doubled as a firewood store and tool shed.

He returned to the shade of the olive tree. The book drew him onward. He wanted to read, even though he had difficulty with the English. He'd never heard of the book until he'd picked it up at the local's pub. A tourist had left it said Maria, the barkeep. Maria explained that the original was written in English but said she'd try to find him a Spanish translation.

No, said Manuel, if the original was in English, he wanted to read the English story. Maria offered to help but he refused, claiming it would be good exercise for his old brain. That was three days ago. Now he didn't want to put the book down. He wanted to know and understand the man's pain in the language of the writer. He'd instinctively suspected that he and the book's fictional character were brothers.

Brothers of the same mother. That he knew as soon as he found the words *la mar*. Brothers. The children of the sea. Yes, he agreed with Santiago, she was a she and not *el mar*. She may be a bitch at times but never a bastard.

Manuel paused - to reflect on all he'd learned so far. He couldn't quite believe just how poor Santiago must've been. But they had so much in common. Manual realised he'd also long stopped dreaming of his long-lost wife. He realised he spoke aloud when he was alone.

Manuel knew he soon had to get himself back to sea. He felt the gnawing urge in his belly, the knotted tugging of pent up nerves. Santiago put him to shame. Imagine, he said to himself, rowing out in the dark before dawn. Rowing out on an empty stomach, not knowing when the next meal would present itself.

I will go to sea again, he told himself. I will find an old wooden boat down in the harbour and fix up. I will paint it bright red, blue and yellow. I will name it *El Campeón* in honour of Santiago. I will do this all before the summer is out. Before the winter storms arrive. I will.

Manuel read until the sun dipped low enough to drive the shadows away from his resting place. It was time to put the book away and stroll down to the local for his evening meal. It was a good thing. He would talk to Maria. She would have answers.

At first Maria wanted nothing to do with his idea of going to sea. No, she said, not even one more time. It was too dangerous for an old man.

He didn't protest at all. He simply said that if she wouldn't help, he'd find someone who would and suggested that she could be a little more helpful. Once she was in agreement things happened quite quickly so even before he'd completed reading the book he'd completed most of his plans and preparations.

He combined his past experience with a few of Santiago's comments. Manual fitted new monofilament braid to his two reels and ensured that his rods were in good order. In his younger days he'd taken great pride in preparing the leaders and traces. Now his fingers quickly found their rhythm. They twisted and turned lines and braids, forming knots, as of old.

He made up a few light handlines for bait fishing. He fished around in a large wooden chest in the tool shed until he found his old leather fishing belt. He carefully checked the stitching and buckles.

"Nothing that a bit of dubbin wouldn't fix."

When his fishing equipment was ship-shape, he packed a backpack with flashlight batteries and dry rations. He would take fresh bread, cheese, ham and fruit on the morning he set out. Oh, and yes, he wouldn't forget to take a few lemons and salt.

He shopped around for a good second-hand outboard motor and fitted out the boat Maria had found for him. He stored spare water, fuel, a few cans of oil and safety gear in the small cabin compartment. He didn't need all this stuff but he knew the harbour folk would stop him from going to sea - if he didn't have everything required by the authorities.

He only had one more detail to wait for before he could set off on his mission. He planned to leave the harbour under the cover of darkness and not wanting to alert anyone of his departure, he needed to do so on the turn of high tide. Yes, he planned to row out, in the dark, just like Santiago had done all those years ago.

He'd have to wait a few days for all the conditions to be in his favour, but he didn't mind. He had the book to keep him company and as he laboured through each page his bond with Santiago grew. He visualised his pain. He imagined being in the skiff for a day and a night while the great fish towed him along.

The afternoon before full moon Manuel went down to the harbour to check the boat one last time. He stowed the book in the hatch for it was his plan to read the last few pages only once he and his friend

Santiago were united at sea. That evening he enjoyed a portion of Maria's fine paella before he headed to the village store to stock up on the fresh supplies.

Manuel didn't sleep much, instead he tossed and turned. Past demons chased him. One, named Tomás, kept screeching at him to run. How could he run? he wondered, he was in a boat at sea. After turning over for what seemed the hundredth time he gave up on sleep. His gut told him it was time to go. It didn't take him long to do his ablutions. Next, he fumbled around in the dark kitchen for his supplies. Breakfast could wait until the sun rose.

He paused for a second or two before closing the front door behind him. Would he return? He didn't know, or care but he thought he'd better greet Aná before going. He stepped back inside and walked to her faded image over the fireplace. He mumbled a few inaudible words of farewell before heading out into the predawn.

The bright full moon lit his path to the harbour. He estimated the time to be somewhere around four, so he knew he'd have enough time to get out of the harbour before the regulars arrived. Once he'd stowed his few additional belongings, he readied the oars and cast off.

He rowed easily, the slack tide offering no resistance. Within half an hour of rowing out past the harbour lights he found the offshore current, so he let the water do the work. The current carried him toward the south west, away from the fast diminishing lights along the *Mallorca* coast. He kept the boat on course with the hand tiller, not bothering with the motor at all.

He ate bread, cheese and ham as he drifted, regretting not bringing a flask of coffee. Oh well, he thought, maybe I won't miss the coffee when the fishing begins. He removed the old mobile phone from his pocket. He carefully removed it from the plastic wrapping. He'd promised Maria that he'd call her once he was away from prying eyes.

"Yes, I am fine. I am drifting out in the channel between *Palma* and *Ibiza*. No, I'm heading south of the islands. Yes, I'll stay around *Illa des Conills* and *Cabrera*. Good… OK, fine. I'll keep in contact, yes, I promise."

He carefully wrapped the phone after switching it off. He stowed it with his other provisions. Now was the time for action. Manuel baited the #4 barbless hooks of the first line with slithers of squid. The second he baited with small cuts of salted sardines. No ordinary salted sardines. He'd spent a few hours preparing these, using one of his old, trusted recipes. Just the correct amount of flavours.

Before casting the lines, he half-filled the bait box with sea water.

"Now… I am ready."

He cast the lines a little way from the boat. One on each side. He felt alive, the most invigourated he had been in many years. His mental race had begun. Him against the fish. This is how it should be, man against the elements.

"I bet the sardines bring the first results."

He spoke aloud, as he knew Santiago would've done. He held each line lightly between thumb and forefinger.

"I wonder if the left hand will fare better that the right? Lefty's holding the sardine line so it should. Yes, I've given the weaker hand the advantage."

Manuel didn't have long to wait. He soon felt the faint twitching of fish nibbling, at both lines. He played the lines, gentle upward movements interspersed with sharper jerks to set the hooks.

"Come on mackerel, swallow your breakfast… yes… yes, and another."

He pulled both lines in simultaneously and stopped as the first fish broke water. He stepped on the left line to hold it in place, allowing him space to remove the fish from each hook of the right line without getting the lines entangled.

"One, two, three and four. Full house on the squid."

He carefully placed each fish in the bait box. The sardine line only yielded three fish.

"Not good lefty, I banked on you and you let me down. Never mind, that was only round one. Three more to go."

He repeated the baiting process and then cast the lines in again, this time he gave the left hand the squid line.

"Got to be fair, no cheating allowed here."

He continued fishing until he'd completed the fourth round. The squid won the day. Thirteen fish to eleven.

"That would do just fine, I now have enough to last me for a day or so. I could even enjoy a bit of raw mackerel as I've got salt and lemon."

Manuel carefully wound up the handlines and stowed them.

"A neat deck is a safe deck."

How long had he known those words? Was it not his father who taught him the saying when he first went to sea?

"A neat deck is a safe deck. Yes, that is so. That is also a lesson I never transferred to my own son, the city boy."

He wistfully shook his head from side to side.

"No, he didn't want to fish, even as a small boy he showed no interest. The little tiddlers in the harbour weren't even inviting."

Manuel stopped himself. This was no time to allow his sorrow to cloud his purpose. This was the time to celebrate the sea. This was the time to unite with Santiago in triumph. The thought of Santiago reminded him of the book. He retrieved it after throwing a quick glance at the sun.

"A good time to rest and read. The sun is high, the big fish will be very deep and not in the mood for eating."

He recalled his days of regular fishing. Most boats would be heading for the harbour by now. Only the tourists stayed out during the high sun. Now was the time to test the motor, he thought. It started easily and got the boat moving smoothly through the water. He headed for the leeward side of *Cabrera*. He would anchor in one of the sheltered bays to lay up until later in the afternoon. He had much to do, the book beckoned.

He found a shady spot under trees close to the beach. He read for a while before dozing off for a few hours. He didn't fight the sleep because he knew he'd need all his strength if he picked up a large fish during the night. He stirred from his slumbers when the sun dipped low enough to cause him discomfort. It took him a few moments to gather his thoughts, but he quickly realised it was time to get going.

Manuel set off toward the south as the sun began its dash toward the horizon. He knew he'd reach the deeper water with enough time remaining to begin his fishing. The mackerel were lively in the bait box because he'd continued refreshing the water. He cut the motor as soon as he established that he was back in the current.

He kept a good lookout for birds and once he thought he saw action further to the south he got the motor going again. No time to row now, he wanted to be in position before dark. He cut the motor when he confirmed that his eyes had not let him down.

"Petrels… the Mother's chickens. You're talking to me, there are fish… I'm sure. Has Saint Santiago sent you to guide me?"

He paused to give this omen a thought. Could it be that the birds are warning him of a storm coming or are they good luck?

"No… you chickens are good, now we fish. Me and Santiago's memory. But… I must first call Maria."

Manuel retrieved the phone, unwrapped it and switched it on. He checked the signal strength before dialling.

"Weak but it will do."

He listened at the ring tone for a few seconds,

"Hello, hello. Yes, I can hear you. No, I'll sleep out on the islands tonight. No, I'm fine. It's warm, I have food and water. No, no… no Maria. Don't be saying that. No, don't send people to look for me. NO! I'm fine. Yes, I'll call… yes, even at night if I need to. Fine. Thanks…

ok, good evening."

Once the phone was stored, he readied his sturdiest rod and real. He chose a 6/0 long shank hook and carefully secured the woven metal leader onto the braid. He checked and rechecked the knots.

He hooked one of the mackerel through the top lip in the classic live bait fashion. He flick-cast the bait out as far from the boat as possible. He kept playing out line until he was satisfied and then set the reel's drag. He pulled at the line while adjusting the setting until he was happy. Then, he placed the rod in the holder and began the wait.

"One rod is good. Don't be greedy… you can only catch one big fish at a time. Eat something and make sure all your gear is in working order. Check your flash light. It will be a little while before the moon rises."

"Eat, old man… eat while you have the time."

He broke chunks of bread and enjoyed some of the ham and cheese. He would first finish off the fresh food and fruit before taking to the dry provisions. He wasn't fond of tinned food but if he stayed out much longer than 48 hours, he would have to keep himself fed with his dry stores.

"Read a little more, before the darkness comes."

He wanted to read but he was distressed by Santiago's plight. Shark after shark was attacking his fish. He marvelled at the resilience and daring of the other man. To fight off the sharks the way he did must have taken so much of his strength.

The descending darkness soon put pay to the reading but the inactivity made him mull over Santiago's fate. He worried that if he should be lucky to catch a big one that he would not be strong enough to handle the fish.

The moon rose an hour after sundown. Manuel enjoyed the beauty.

"It's been so long since I've seen such a splendid sight. Even if I catch no fish this makes it worthwhile."

The boat drifted slowly toward the south west. He thought he could still make out the distant low-lying outline of the islands. There was no action on the rod so around midnight he reeled in the line to replace the bait.

The mackerel wasn't in good shape. Many small mouths had nibbled at the fish.

"Just as well I checked. You're no good anymore. I'll hook up one of your brothers"

Manuel rebaited the hook and cast out the line again. He played out less line this time. He didn't want to spend half the night retrieving line. Once he'd set the reel's tension and replaced the rod in the stand, he made himself comfortable.

"I may as well doze off… the reel will wake me if a fish runs with the bait."

He slept in fits and starts, waking every so often. His subconscious was looking out for him. He checked the line and the boat's drift to make sure all was well. The moon and stars told their tale. He would eventually land up in Algeria if he kept going on this current. He'd have to make a call by early morning to start the motor and head in a homeward direction.

The reel woke him in the predawn. The ratchet click-clicking a few times before he could knock it off. He placed a fingertip loosely on the line, feeling the slight tremors coming back at him. He waited for signs of a full run but it didn't come. The fish had dropped the bait.

"Come on fish… don't let me down."

He waited a few more minutes before retrieving the line.

"Son of a syphilitic seafaring sailor… you took my bait and not my hook. Let me get another bait on there…"

He hurriedly rebaited and cast in again. This time he didn't bother to let more than 50 meters of line out before returning the rod to the holder. It seemed to him as if the boat's drift had slowed down. He dipped his hand into the water to feel the flow.

"Yes… I think we've slowed so the bait will sink too deep if I let out lots of line."

He glances toward the east. A faint showing of colour confirmed the impending arrival of a new day.

"Come on fish, this is your time to feed. You don't feed deep down in the dark so get back to your snack, won't you?"

He didn't have long to wait. He was about the get the last of the fresh food ready for breakfast when the reel wound into action. The rod tip arched as the fish began its run.

"Oh ho… give me a minute fish! I need my belt… I can't tame you without help."

Manuel suddenly regretted being out alone. How would he handle the boat and the fish at the same time?

"Be good to me fish… please let me off kindly and I'll be good to you. Please?"

Once he'd strapped on the belt he lifted the rod. The fish was still taking line but he knew he'd soon have to begin applying more pressure, if he wanted any chance of turning the fish.

"Don't empty the reel fish… then I'll never get you in."

He slowly tightened the drag… while pulling back on the rod. The line was running off to the side of the boat causing cross drag. It could work in his favour, but it could just as easily put too much resistance on the line. He began reeling in, slowly, as gently as the fish would allow. He knew he'd have to use the boat as a break but how much pressure could he apply?

"Experience… let your experience take over…"

Slowly, very slowly, he began winning back line. He made his way to the bow so that the fish could pull against as little resistance if it should turn again. He had to be very careful not to be pulled off the small bow deck.

"Old man, what are you doing. You'll fall overboard and become food for the fish."

He kept working the fish until he noticed the fish was towing him back toward the islands, directly into the rising sun. He also noticed the line seemed to be rising. He knew he'd have to be ready for the fish to turn and run again as they usually do when they surface.

He kept the rod tip high and made the decision to head back to use the rod holder. He needed a rest and the best way to do so was to use the motor to follow the fish for a while.

"Fish, you have me between the devil and the dark blue, that you have. Either I take a chance and put you in the rod holder or you wear me out and I lose you."

He tied a short rope strop loop above the reel and then to a cleat on the gunwale.

"Stay where you are rod."

Manuel loosened the drag just enough to slacken the excessive arc in the rod. He hoped he'd be able to reel in line quick enough while steering the boat toward the fish. He started the motor and put it into gear. He set the throttle - the boat crept forward just enough for him reel in line.

"Fish… don't play any tricks. Be good to me and I'll be good to you. I promise!"

He kept creeping toward the east, toward the fish. Instinct told him he'd chanced his arm enough. He stopped the motor, loosened the tie-down and lifted the rod.

"I must eat, I need my strength and I must phone Maria. She will worry."

He inched his way toward the hatch to get the phone and food. He was about to reach for the phone when he felt the shudder in the line. That shudder alerted him to danger. The danger of the fish outwitting him.

"Are you coming up to show yourself? Yes… you want to show

me your size. You want to let me see who's boss."

He'd retrieved most of the line so he expected to see the fish near the boat. He wasn't ready for the size and beauty of the fish. Although the fish didn't quite break the surface, he could see the shimmering neon cobalt blue glistening just below the surface. It was the biggest bluefin tuna he'd ever seen. The fish must be all of three meters, he thought.

"Fish, I will not harm you, I will not let them sell you and eat you raw. You are too beautiful."

The fish seemed to look him in the eye and as Manuel expected, he turned and dived straight down, the great tail momentarily breaking water as it scythed its way downward.

Manuel was as ready as he could be. He'd slackened off the drag as much as possible to allow the fish a partially free run. He kept the rod tip as high as possible. He used the precious few moments to reach for the phone, using his teeth to unwrap the plastic.

He concentrated on the rod tip and the line's tension while getting the phone switched on. As soon as he was sure he had signal he quick-dialled Maria. She must have been holding the phone because she answered on the second ring.

"Good morning… yes, I'm fine. No, I need help."

He listened to Maria's panicked response.

"No… I've had an idea. Get the people from the oceanarium to come out and help me. Yes… the researchers. I have a massive bluefin on the line."

He listened while she repeated what he'd just said to whoever was listening. He heard someone in the background say he'd call the oceanarium immediately. Yes, he knew one of the main men there. It took him a second to realise Maria was again speaking to him.

"Oh, I'm out south of the islands. Yes, I can see them on the horizon. I'm sure I see *Puig Major* far to the north east. I must go. I'll leave the phone on. I'll try to answer but the fish needs my attention, *now*."

He realised he'd lost sight of what he and the fish were doing and that he'd have to concentrate on the battle otherwise he would lose his prize after all the effort they'd both put in.

He again went through the long process of regaining lost line. The fish came grudgingly. On more than one occasion he could feel line thumps.

"He's shaking his head… he wants to be free. Wait fish… I'll let you go when the time is right."

The ringing phone startled him. He answered as soon he could. It was a male voice.

"Yes? Oh good. Yes, the fish is still fighting strongly. He's run twice."

Manuel listened to the man on the other end of the line. They were a crew from the oceanarium who'd slept over on the island, so they were close by. Yes, they were well on the way. Did he have flares? Fine… they'd ring when they thought they were close enough to see. He was lucky, said the man.

Lucky? No, not lucky, rather fated. The omens were with him. Santiago had sent the Mother's chickens as a sign. The fish will be his and he'd keep his promise. Santiago knew that and would honour his desire to bring the fish in.

Manuel managed to get the fish alongside the boat again. They stared at each other for another brief moment… before the fish put its head down and set off on another run. This time he was more prepared and didn't bother trying to handle the boat and the fish. The boat would follow as long as he allowed the fish its freedom to move.

The fish slowed and he began the retrieval of line again.

"You're getting tired fish… you haven't run so far this time. You've left much line on the reel."

Manuel was grateful that the fish was tiring. He was nearing exhaustion as well.

"Come people, I need your help."

He realised he'd not spoken aloud this time, as if he feared the fish hearing him admitting to being almost beaten. No, I mustn't give up. Santiago didn't, even though he'd been much more exhausted.

"But Santiago missed having the boy to help him so he must have suffered terribly. I will have help. I will manage."

Then, to his joy, the phone rang. They asked if he would shoot a flare and cut the call. Manuel placed the rod in the holder and tied it off. The tension should keep the fish happy. Then he looked through the survival gear until he found a red 1000-foot flare. He removed it from its canister, pulled the safety pin and set it off.

He watched as the flare whooshed upward. He hoped it wouldn't spook the fish.

The phone rang almost immediately. They confirmed that they had seen his flare and would be with him in about 15 minutes. Good, now he could concentrate on the fish – as he should.

The fish allowed him to bring in almost all the line before it turned and headed out again. This time it stayed near the surface so Manuel suspected it may be the last run.

"Soon… you'll be mine and soon you'll be free. Soon, I promise."

The run was a short one and he was winning line again when he first heard the thumping of the research vessel's diesels.

"We'll both rest - soon fish, of that I'm sure."

He recognised the voice calling out from the other boat.

"What do you want us to do?"

"What do you usually do when you catch large bluefins?"

"We bring them on board in a sling... we do our measurements and take samples. We tag the fish and then we release them."

Manuel watched as the boat took up station behind his boat. They kept a fair distance so as not to snag his line.

"Don't you want to capture the fish and sell him? You'll make a lot of money."

"No! I promised the fish he'll go free."

"Fantastic. We don't get to see such lovely specimens often anymore. Here's what we'll do. Two of the team will swim to your boat and help you while we get you transferred over to our boat. Then we'll sling the fish when it's ready and bring him on board."

Manuel watched the two men dive in and swim over. A shudder on the line reminded him that he needed to concentrate on the fish and not on the men.

The men made easy work of getting onto Manuel's boat.

"Here's what we'll do. You keep playing the fish while we steer your boat to the rear of ours... then we'll help you across onto the swim platform while you keep control of the fish. One of the other team members will help you onto our boat's deck."

Manuel was surprised how easily the transfer happened. Fortunately, the sea was calm. Within minutes he was sitting in a fighting chair on the research vessel. The men on his boat then steered it away from the area.

"How are you holding up?"

Manuel looked at the team leader.

"What's your name young man?"

"Forgive my rudeness, it's Luis."

"The fish is almost ready so what will we do when he comes up?"

"Come around to the rear of the boat when you're ready. We'll have the sling prepared on the swim platform."

Manuel kept bringing in line until he had the fish almost on the surface. He maneuvered the fish alongside the swim platform and watched as the team worked skilfully to get the sling beneath the fish. Luis took up the slack on the straps connected to the sling's anchor points.

"On my signal, place the reel in free spool and we'll lift the fish with the derrick."

The men steadied the sling as it cleared the water.

"Ok, now."

Manuel released the spool as Luis began hoisting the fish upward. Once he'd swung it onto the deck the men worked fast. One put a hose in the fish's mouth and covered its head with a wet cloth while another kept hosing flowing water on the fish's skin.

"We cover the eyes and flow fresh water over the gills and the skin. Now we can work on the fish because it will remain docile as long as it can't see what's going on."

Luis noticed Manuel was still holding the rod.

"Put down your rod Manuel, the fight is over."

"So it is. I'm very tired."

"You can rest very soon. First, come join me here at the head. I want you to hold the tape measure so we can get photos of you and your fish."

Manuel watched the team at work. One handed him the tape while another held the other end in the V of the tail. Luis showed him where to hold his end.

"Three point zero five meters. Wow, indeed a unique catch. I don't think anyone has landed a fish this size in the Mediterranean in many a year. Come, let's get a few photos of you holding the tape."

"Luis, may I ask a favour please?"

"By all means, what can we do?"

"I have a book on my boat, can your men please bring it over?"

Luis immediately hailed the men to bring Manuel's boat closer. While they waited for Manuel's boat to come alongside Luis instructed the men to tag the fish.

"We double tag this beauty. The one is a pop-up satellite tag that will relay its data when it's released. The other tag is a newer long-term device. We inject it under the skin between the two dorsal fins. We believe the tags have a better chance of remaining intact there."

When Manuel's boat came alongside, he explained what he was after. One of the men retrieved the book and passed it across to Luis who handed it to Manuel.

"Will you now take the photo please?"

Luis took a few photos from different angles while Manuel held the end of the tape measure in one hand and the book in the other.

"That is good, now we better get the fish back into the water - to minimise its stress."

"Luis, why do you not put this fish in the large tank at the oceanarium? That way the people will see its beauty."

"We would love to… but it will most likely just be its death sentence. Big tuna don't like aquariums, they usually die soon after being put into tanks. It's worth much more out in the wild with the tracking tags giving us valuable data on its behaviour."

The team lowered the fish back into the water. They allowed the it to stay in the loosened sling, for support, until it recovered sufficiently to make its escape. Manuel watched with the team as the fish dived out of sight.

"Go free my friend, live long!"

"Manuel, you have done a great thing today. We hope to get years of information from your fish. What shall we call him? Manuel… or another name?"

"Tomás… someone I knew long ago."

Luis noticed a hint of melancholy in Manuel's tone but he knew it would be out of place to ask.

"We shall do that. Now, let's get you back to *Port de Campos*. We'll tow your boat, you rest."

Manuel sat in the fighting chair, staring out at the ocean for a long while. One of the men brought him a mug of sweet coffee which he sipped slowly. He found himself muttering beneath his breath.

"He was a dream. I didn't see him but in my dreams. Better a dream that lives on than the dead skeleton lashed to a skiff. I am happy that you live fish. You are too beautiful to die by man's hand."

He slept well that night and woke the next morning to realise he'd become an overnight local hero. Maria brought him the newspapers. His photo was all over the front pages.

In a Madrid skyscraper office another man sat looking at the article. The man couldn't contain his bitter frustration any longer.

"It's time to return home. It's time to leave this empty life behind and go back to the islands."

The man couldn't quite make out what the fisherman held in his left hand. He turned to his laptop and opened the national daily's webpage. Then, he enlarged the front page photo.

"He got his inspiration from a book."

He enlarged the photo a little more.

"Ernest Hemingway… *The Old Man and the Sea.*"

Tomás sighed a deep, almost sorrowful sigh.

"Now, I'll go and learn about inspiration from my father, if he'll still have me."

My Father

My father's only contribution to my existence was the infusion of sperm into my mother's apparently less than willing receptacle. That, I learned as life went on, was according to my mother and her family, the sum total of their fleeting encounter.

Yes, I'd arrived in the world without the paternal support deemed so necessary for the wholesome character formation of men children. Abiding memories of my early childhood centred around one central theme.

My legitimacy.

Adults whispered, children whispered. Everybody whispered. At first, I was totally oblivious of all the carry-on. That's to be expected, you'd have to agree. After all, all I cared about then was getting a good feed from the two moon balloon protrusions attached to my mother's chest. That and having long, slow dumps. Those things seemed to be the only important matters in life. Oh, apparently sleep was near the top of the list as well.

So, why did I care that adults and children were whispering? Life was good, I got to hang off her ample boobs and dump. And sleep. However, as these things go in life, I couldn't remain in that state forever.

Soon I was crawling about the place. Life was still good. I still got to do my three most favourite things in life while other pleasures were added to my already hectic schedule. Playing in water was the next best discovery. Oh, don't let me forget projectile peeing. I loved catching anyone, who came within range, off guard.

One of my mother's many sisters would remind me (for most of my adult life) of my unnerving knack of getting adults in the face. Yep, my little member seemingly reacted on instinct as soon as it was exposed to fresh air. Not much has changed, these days it still reacts when exposed to fresh air… and female flesh.

Life moved on. Soon they sent me off to school with a few of my cousins. One or two of them were my best friends. Make that two of them. They were my best friends only because they were family and had to suffer the indignation of having to be my friends. It seemed even that early in life that there was something amiss with me.

People whispered. Incessantly. As soon as I appeared people drew closer together. The whispers were always preceded by furtive glances in my direction. Another anomaly that occurred with regular frequency was the effect that adults had on their children. Usually, just moments after their whispering began they'd vacate the room with their little Johnnie's and Jane's in tow.

You can imagine my confusion. I was just a timid little boy but they all seemed to be afraid of me.

Why?

Then, one day, the answer arrived unexpectedly. I overheard snippets of a conversation. Two of the class bullies were discussing my ailment without realising I was within earshot. One said to the other,

"My mother says his mother is a whore."

"Why?"

"Because he has no father."

"Why?"

"I don't know stupid, but my mother says."

Boy, was I happy to hear those words. I wanted to befriend the bullies there and then. They'd solved my life's most pressing dilemma. Wow, was I happy. Now I knew what was wrong with me. Well, actually, there seemed to be nothing wrong with me. It seemed that my mother's condition was to blame for my predicament.

I probably smiled for the rest of the day. I couldn't remember ever being so happy for so long. I couldn't wait to get home to share my newfound knowledge with my mother. I didn't understand but at least I now knew why everyone whispered.

I ran home after school. I could no longer contain my excitement. I hoped my mother would be there to meet me but I was disappointed. Only my grandparents were around. I waited the agonizing hours for my mother's return. We were all together. What a perfect moment for me. There we were, at the dinner table. I was so happy. I was with the three people around which my planet revolved.

My grandpa said grace. A long prayer of thanksgiving. Later in life, I learned that the longer his prayers the less he looked forward to the fare on his plate. If he was in a hurry to eat he'd only mutter a few short sentences. It was his ploy. The longer he prattled on the bigger his excuse. The food was cold; he didn't like cold food so my granny would have to make him something else.

That evening he mumbled on and on. I opened one eye to peep. My mother's eyes were closed. Her serene look added to her beauty. Yes, my mother. She must have been the best whore on the planet, I thought. I chose my moment with care, wanting all three the adults to have my full attention when I asked the question that had been eating at me that whole day.

The meal eventually drew to a close. Moments before my grandpa gave the signal to excuse me, I popped my question.

"Mommy, why didn't you ever tell me you were a whore?"

I must say, their collective reaction wasn't at all what I'd expected… or hoped for. How was I supposed to know my simple query was going to get me a tongue lashing of epic proportion?

My mother's exasperated wail sounded almost primeval, a jackal bitch howling at the Southern Cross.

"Whaaaat?"

She fled, her sobs bouncing off the hall walls as she retreated.

My grandpa took control of the situation. At first he spoke softly but with each passing sentence the intensity of his tones increased. By the time he'd corrected my perception of the word whore he was almost shouting.

"A whore is a bad woman, one who takes men to places they don't belong… places of pain. A whore will prey on unwitting men. A whore will do their evil on the unexpected. Your mother is not a whore and never was a whore."

I remember, even as a small boy, wondering why he got so uptight if my mother hadn't in some way contributed to gaining the label. I also remember never quite shaking the feeling that I'd done permanent damage to the relationship with my grandparents.

It eventually took the soft spoken, gentle intervention of my granny to calm the old man down.

"Stop now, you've made your point. Have you considered, even for a moment, that the lad doesn't know what the word means?"

That shut the insufferable old fool up. My granny had come to the rescue, again. Something else happened that day. I realised that she'd be my ally while I was growing up. Not my mother, rather my granny.

Fortunately, the whore incident took place on a Friday. The next day my granny took me to the park. It was her way of getting me away from the house to explain the situation.

"Those two bully boys were just spreading gossip. Your father died before you were born. Some people started a rumour that your mother was not good, that she had done wrong and that's why you came along. They never knew the whole story."

My little mind was even more scrambled. A father that dies, how? Granny explained that he'd died in a car crash.

"You know that old wreck in the rear garden at your aunt's house? That was the car."

From that day I never ever set foot in that garden again. From that day I simply didn't bother to wonder about my mother's status. The whispers hurt but by the time I started secondary school I didn't care anymore. Actually, I stopped caring about much and went on to become a reclusive, difficult man who could only find a spiritual home within the fighting forces. The army was the answer. They wanted silent, strong individuals who didn't ask questions and didn't complain about the hard life imposed on Special Forces.

Oh, I mustn't forget to mention… women. Yes, I became an off-duty whore chaser. I needed the release… the revenge, some would say. Whatever way you want to put it, I was on my one-man mission to get even. That experience, as a six-year-old, was ingrained. I would try and lay every girl I could. As the old army adage went, *find em, fornicate and forget em!!*

Then, one day while I was home on leave, a strange request arrived. My aunt asked if I wanted to meet my father.

Meet who… my *dead* father? Were we going to have a séance?

I refused at first but the more I thought about it the more intrigued I became. Meet my father?

"Ok, I'll consider a meeting but first you'll have to fill me in on a few facts, not myths."

That was all I needed to say to my aunt. She understood my need to know what had happened in my early childhood. Only when fact was separated from fiction could I make up my mind.

Now, here I sat while a lifetime of memories lashed through my over excited brain. What would my mother say if she saw me now? Would she be proud or would she turn away now as she did when I was a little boy?

I shook my head from side to side. An involuntary reaction, in an attempt to clear the massed jumble of thoughts.

"Show me the moist, receptive fanny that refuses willy and I'll show you the dark side of the moon."

My father's words banged loud and clear in the confused grey space seconding as my brain. The words echoed, rebounding off the bone walls, amplifying the churning torrents of emotion.

I looked down. A serene peace overcame me. My mind drifted back to the day I met my father. The day I first heard his words of wisdom.

"Show me the moist, receptive fanny that refuses willy and I'll show you the dark side of the moon."

That first meeting had been a rather tense affair. Well, the first few minutes, as I recall. After I'd overcome my initial impulse to strike him down I realised we may have some catching up to do.

He was quick to assure me that he hadn't paid my mother for the act of inseminating her. He then went on to inform me that once he found out about my impending arrival he'd made it his business to contribute financially.

"So yes, in a way you could say your mother was a whore. I kept paying, year in and year out, until you'd earned your first month's pay."

My noncommittal reaction spurred him on. It was his turn to vent. All the years of bottled up frustration boiled over.

"That pig-headed old man who called himself your grandfather banished me from your life but didn't mind the monthly funds arriving in your mother's bank account."

As time went by we built quite a relationship. Shared fishing trips, sports events, even the odd music festival. We found each other. Only problem? Just as I was becoming human, he went and croaked on me. You'll have to agree with me, such a loss was enough to send any man back into his solitary world.

Then my phone rang. It was Lucy, an occasional liaison. Her sobs drove home the reason for her call. Pregnant. Bloody hell, how on earth could that have happened? Easy lad, easy. Remember your father's words?

"Show me the moist, receptive fanny that refuses willy and I'll show you the dark side of the moon."

Lucy, an aspiring lawyer, didn't want to be burdened with the restraints of baby raising. OK, said I, if the paternity test proves I'm to blame then I'll raise the child. So… the wait was on. The little bundle arrived in the early hours of a wild, stormy summer's night. Appropriate?

The test results confirmed my contribution, so… I'd become the proud owner of a human dependent. Don't get me wrong, I was proud! This intervention in the rhythm of life would be my way of proving to my mother and father's memory that I had what it took to be a man.

The military helped. My aunt helped. The neighbours helped. I was amazed, when it dawned on me, just how human folks could be. I'd be a fool to say the whole experience of becoming a father didn't change me. It did. For the better.

Tempest Moon, I named her. The little bundle of joy galvanised the folk in my immediate world. For the first time in my life I had a purpose and a bright one at that. My only regret in the whole brightening in my life was that my father wasn't there to see his granddaughter.

Tempest Moon. In honour of my father's famous dark side quip and her arrival on the totally out of character stormy summer's night.

My father. The man who shaped me. My father, he who was always in the distant background even though I only found that out when I was well into my mid-twenties.

Here I sat, looking down at the next instalment of the saga. The next twist. Here I was sitting in a maternity ward, again. Here I was, looking down at the next instalment in life's saga. A beautiful bundle of joy. Tempest Moon's own little daughter. Here I was, grateful to be a grandfather and looking forward to being as much a part of both their lives as my own mother never was in mine.

My father's words were ringing in my ears, as they had in the past they were now reminding me of my responsibility in the upkeep of the cycle of life.

"Show me the moist, receptive fanny that refuses willy and I'll show you the dark side of the moon."

The Dead Pussy Society

Her chest heaved… uncontrollably. Her breathing laboured and rasping. She raised her right arm, hand reaching for unfathomed truths of the twilight. She thought, for a fleeting second, she understood why so many violent crimes were committed under the blanket of darkness. She was a jealous lover, never wanting others to see her prize. *Her* prize!

She panted… deep, irregular pulses. She was acutely aware that the next minute or two would be the making or breaking of her future. She was also acutely aware that 25 eyes were boring into her back. Twelve apostles and the one-eyed Underworldling didn't for a second cast their gaze elsewhere. They were all staring into her future. Would she fulfil her destiny and complete the sacrificial calling?

She felt the muscles in her torso drawing tauter at every breath. Her right arm ached, the strain of holding it aloft even for the short few moments resulted in overstretched sinews and tendons feeling as if they were about to tear into millions of blood splattered fragments.

The low chanting from behind intensified until the wash of the low growl ebbed and flowed rhythmically with her every breath.

"Pussy, *pussy*… dead pu-*ssy!* Dead pusssssss-yyyyy… deaaaaaad PU-*SSY!!*"

She paused, letting the atmosphere sweep her toward her climax. She thrust again, carnal feelings of lusty avarice intensifying by the second. This, she groaned, was the beginning of her reign. She knew that within seconds she'd fulfil her life's calling. A long road… a long road trodden with planning and purpose after she'd discovered the Society. Or, had the Society discovered her?

The Society, now her society. What an accomplishment. The years of preparation, the years of training. The years of living for this moment. This moment of fulfilment which had begun almost twenty years ago when she'd been asked a seemingly innocent question. Her memories of the past crystalised in the intensity of the erotic moments of the ceremony.

"Billy, you know *Nebraska Peace*… the Yellow Hawks song?"

She sighed,

"Yes Georgy, of course I know the song. Why? Did you think I'm fresh in from the moon?"

Georgy ignored her barb. He was so used to his best friend's sharp tongue that it didn't get to him anymore. Billy was Billy and if you didn't like the way she did things she'd discard you quicker than a twice used teabag. He carried on regardless.

"The song ends with words something along this line… *you're welcome anytime to play but forever you'll have to stay!"*

He paused, keeping his gaze fixed on the earth. They were in their forest hideout, surrounded by Mother Nature's embrace. The dappled, diffused light cast strange shadows on the ground. He continued doodling in the hard-baked earth with the stick he'd been toying with.

"You can never leave. Do you get it? Never. Once you've been accepted there is no way out. Well, two ways, one to kill the Supreme One and the other is death. Actually, it's one and the same thing… legend says, you kill the Supreme One and you'll be dead before the next sunrise."

Only then had Georgy looked up at her. She recalled the angst in his eyes. She recalled his confused mannerisms, his pained, hesitant words.

"Billy, I love you… you're my best friend… even though you don't want me I still love you."

The words tumbled out of Georgy, random spewings, the products of a pained and confused mind.

"I don't want you to get hurt. Never. The only thing, if you join, you'll be tied, never is an eternity you know."

"Georgy, I know you love me. We're the same age, we're young. Only seventeen. All the love stuff can wait. You know I'm up for joining. I know what must get done. I know the Society almost never accepts girls or women. *I know!"*

She'd moved closer to him and placed her arm around his shoulders. She was the leader, already at this point she knew it was her destiny. She'd gently stroked his hair and soothed him, like a mother would a baby.

"Georgy, do you love me or is it only the novelty of you having a best friend who's hot? Is it me or my body?"

She thought he was going to cry. She was certain she could feel tremors spreading through his body.

"Georgy, maybe you can share my body but you'll never have my mind. That is only mine. No one will ever take that from me."

Georgy sat in stunned silence. The whole episode seemed so surreal. His best friend wanted to join an almost exclusive male fraternity. The brotherhood would now cease to exist as such. As much as he loved her it just seemed wrong that she should be allowed into their exclusive realm.

Worse still, Georgy suspected she knew exactly how split his emotions and feelings actually were. He wanted her, he craved her. He longed to touch her, to feel her soft girlhood. Womanhood? Whatever-hood. He could feel the warmth in his groin growing, so much so that he had to shift position to accommodate the swelling mass.

"Georgy, if you want to see my body I'll show you. I'll let you touch me… even stroke and caress me. I'd like that."

Billy remembered the day as if she was living the moment now. That was the first time she'd used her body to get something she wanted. She'd wanted Georgy to get her an audience with the Chapter Master. She wanted to be accepted into the Society.

She'd stripped for him, slowly, enticingly… drawing out his pain. She'd remained just out of his reach for quite a few minutes. Teasing, gently teasing. Then she'd stepped directly up to him. Her midriff aligned with his face. She placed her hands on his shoulders, ensuring he remained seated on the log.

She allowed him to run his hands all along her flanks. His touch slightly rough at first but she kept speaking softly, instructing him, guiding his hands with her words. She sensed more than saw his gaze fixed on her mound. The tingling grew as he caressed. His hands moved over her firm breasts.

Billy kept whispering and Georgy kept caressing. His soft moaning intensified until he could contain himself no longer. She felt his one hand leaving her inner thigh. She watched as he hastily undid his trousers. He sighed as his hard member broke from its restraints. She could see the wetness shimmering on the tip.

She caught herself. He was big. He looked so strong but no, she wanted no part in his manhood. Not yet, at least. She allowed him to play with himself while he kept caressing her inner thighs. Then she felt his tongue gently parting her lips. He probed, primeval instincts taking over the control of his tongue.

In a blur those memories of almost two decades ago rushed back. She and Georgy, her man servant for all these years. She'd allowed others access to her body but it was only ever her best friend Georgy who she'd allowed to bring her to fulfilment. Her Georgy.

Much had happened in the intervening years. She'd been granted her audience with the Chapter Master. Not long after that she'd been granted acceptance. The initiation ritual hadn't fazed her in the least. She broke the kitten's neck with one sharp twist. After all, she'd been reminded, she couldn't join the Dead Pussy Society without accomplishing the basic entry requirement.

She'd learned more and more of the Society's history as time passed. Well over two hundred years in existence, some suggested. Some went as far as to say two hundred and fifty. They looked after each other. They invested in each other's businesses and promoted the wellbeing of fellows.

They swayed the views of politicians and quietly persuaded local and regional leaders to implement change, to the benefit of the members in particular and society in general. They were the silent backbone in most communities.

Occasionally, rumours wafted in the undergrowth about clandestine trade-offs. Sometimes the general public couldn't understand a particular politician's stand on a community matter but it went without saying that their interests were usually well catered for. The general rank and file population knew nothing about the organisation. The media never seemed to get any leads. Maybe because virtually every editor belonged firmly in the Society's pockets.

There was much for Billy to learn about the administration of the Society. She was a natural organiser, so it didn't take long for her to rise in the ranks. She dragged Georgy with her. She soon travelled far and wide, attending different Chapters, organising, communicating and most of all, always growing.

All the while she had Georgy for back up. No one tried to mess with her. She had the unspoken protection of the Upper Counsel, even though she at first didn't have a clue who they were. She'd been informed that a particular lady had her back. Apparently the only other female serving at that time.

Then the summons arrived. She was still in her early twenties when she first met Felicity. The Fox, as she was known within the Society.

"How far do you intend going in the Society?"

"All the way… to the very top, then a little further."

"Well lass, here are ground rules. Number one, never marry. I was married when I was approached to join. That means I can never become the Supreme One."

The Fox paused at that point, intently studying Billy's face, looking for any sign of flinching.

"Good, I take it you've not let your heart go."

"I have… to a degree but he knows he can only have my body. He knows we'll never be married."

"Right, next on your list, if you want to reach the top. You'll have to create a stronger persona. I know the whispers abound that you're a mean lady. I know there's talk that you'd chew up most anybody before breakfast but you have to become a ballbreaker."

"What do you suggest I do?"

"Patience Billy, patience. First, you need to take a lover. A woman."

Again she watched Billy's reaction. Again she saw no sign of weakness.

"That seems like a pleasant challenge. May I keep Georgy in the background? He's been *my* boy since just before we turned eighteen."

"Yes, you may but be very discreet because your lover is going to be me."

The Fox licked her lips in as a seductive way as she could manage. She was looking forward to the pleasure and she wasn't shy to show it. She could hardly contain her laugh.

"Seems my whole destiny has been mapped. I'm looking forward to the ride, the rougher and stormier the better."

An exaggerated heaving gasp for breath dragged her back to the present. Soon her moment would arrive. She was so near the point of perfection she could hardly contain the spasms gathering strength in her groin. Sweat trickled down her forehead, stinging her eyes. Her vision blurred, obscuring the fine young female figure of Autumn on the ceremonial alter before her.

Slow moaning whimpers escaped Autumn's half open mouth. They were coupled, her rhythmic motions transferring to the youth's delicate body.

"No… wait for me… wait."

Her left hand caressed the youth's flat belly, her motions involuntary. Billy seemed to drift in and out of consciousness… in and out of the past. Bittersweet memories of dark days in the past drifted by.

Her relationship with The Fox had grown into a very tight working affair. They occasionally enjoyed each other's beds but mostly it was business. The Fox taught her all there was to know. The ins and outs, the financial empire's hidden secrets. The backdoors to the vaults, the front doors to success.

Billy learned to manipulate money from place to place… country to country, from commodity to stock, all the while swelling the Society chests. She learned and as she grew in confidence and character she was allowed deeper into the heart of the organisation.

Not long after meeting The Fox she was instructed to take Georgy aside and plot his future's course.

She'd flown down to the east coast and met Georgy for a weekend getaway. Sometime during the weekend she'd sat him down for a one on one.

"Georgy, it's time you marry. Very soon."

The image flashed past… the abject horror in his eyes, that picture will remain with her for life.

"No Georgy, you're not losing me, I'll always be there for you. Always. You will never be left out of my life."

"Why must I marry someone then?"

"Let's just say the planning is for me to move on up in the ranks and away from the hometown. Your role is to remain and fulfil your duties, some of which include providing the Society with offspring."

She sat watching the poor, sobbing man. She drew him near and did what she always did for Georgy. She soothed his ragged nerves in the way he yearned. Her physical touch soon drew the angst from his soul.

"Your key role in the Society will become much clearer in the years to come."

Before checking out of the hotel she'd handed him a slip of paper. It contained three names.

"Those three men are local to your area. As you can guess, they are Chapter members. Each have a daughter of dating age. Visit all three of them before you make your selection but don't dally."

She pecked him on the cheek before turning to walk away.

"Oh, don't forget to invite me to your wedding. You'll find the father of the bride will be only too happy to have me at the head table."

The invitation card duly arrived a few months later. She'd spent the whole night before his wedding with him, soothing, always soothing. Georgy was terrified that she would turn her back on him once he'd been with another woman. She'd calmed his stormy fears and allayed his doubts.

The wedding was a roaring success. She was even allowed a few dances with the groom. She met little Miss Georgy, a sweet, petite ginger. Billy could see what he found attractive in her. She'd make him happy and give him a good time and offspring. He'd keep climbing the Society ranks with her at his side. However, his away from home business trips would be an entirely different matter; that she would ensure.

Her rise was meteoric. Within fifteen years she'd caught glimpses of the inner echelons of power. Power that crossed boundaries, power that arranged deaths or helped people disappear.

Billy kept Georgy happy whenever they could meet. His children were growing up fast. Autumn, his eldest turned sixteen only days before Georgy's wife disappeared. Georgy understood, the drink had driven her away.

All the while Felicity continued her grooming. She'd been chosen. Selected to lead.

"Do you ever wonder when your day will come? Do you ever

wonder why you've been chosen?"

"I've presumed the Supreme One must step down. I've presumed it was always my destiny to lead but I've never tried to answer the why question. A select few are born to it, this new royalty of ours."

"Yes, and you are one of the very few selected for destiny's call."

"Why?"

"To be honest, I'm not entirely sure if this is truth or myth but there's a rumour circulating that you're the Supreme One's daughter."

Billy allowed herself the slightest moment's hesitation before her sharp intake of breath.

"Leadership runs in the family then, it seems."

"Yes, and so does responsibility."

"I know, oh how I know... you've taught me so well I feel I could march on into infinity, always successfully taking on the next challenge."

Felicity admired Billy's dash and daring. Yes, she admitted to herself, there must be truth in the rumour that she'd been ordained to be the Supreme One's heir because she was his daughter.

Felicity also knew she'd have to complete Billy's preparation soon.

"Billy, there are a few rumours within the Society that you may have come to hear in the last few years."

"Yes, I've heard the whispers. Two in particular. One seems to be quite reasonable but the other may be farfetched."

"Share your news and I'll confirm or deny..."

"The first... the Supreme One never just goes off into the sunset, a new Supreme One can only be elected and inaugurated when the incumbent passes on."

"Correct."

Billy remained silent, not sure she wanted to share the second rumour because it seemed a little too much to expect of anyone. The Fox allowed the silence to drag on.

"OK, if you're not ready to share the second bit of information at this point we can move on."

"Thanks, give me a day or two to think it over but I have a strong feeling your words have indicated that there is truth in the second rumour."

"Mind you, you'll be meeting the Supreme One within days... all should become much clearer then, I would guess."

"That's news, why haven't you shared that titbit with me before now?"

"There's a time for everything... now is the time for you to begin your final steps toward the pinnacle."

The thoughts and memories churned through Billy's heightened state of almost ecstasy. The dim light is the Society's underground vault mingled with the smoke swirling off the damp rosewood coals. She knew the climax was near but the belt seemed to have slipped, causing her heightened sensation to turn to friction.

Her aching muscles refocused her energy. She'd have to lower her extended right arm. Soon. She moved the strap-on as best she could with her left hand. She was aware of the eyes boring into her lithe muscles. Only two sets of those eyes had ever had the privileged of seeing her naked splendour.

Georgy, her man servant and Felicity, her mentor stood side by side with the other elders. Now their lifelong destinies became one. The new Supreme One was about to ascend the throne of the Society's kingdom.

"The responsibility of ultimate power… the power of ultimate responsibility…"

The words of the Supreme One rang true as a bell in her head. The words seemed to float on the air… on the smoke… the words mingled with the defused light, further adding to enchantment in the cavernous rock lair.

A vision of the Supreme One's face danced before her mind's eye.

"You'll have a responsibility to the Society. The responsibility of life and death will be in your hands. You'll have to reward Georgy for his sacrifice. You must grant him life for the one that must end. He's been your rock and support… now he'll fulfil your needs for an heir."

At that moment of her meeting with the Supreme One she'd finally understood. Yes, the rumours were true. A life for the ascendency. The life of a young virgin, that's what was expected of her. It was the way of the Society… the death of a pussy.

"The Underworldling will see to all the details… the ceremonial feast will take place within weeks of my passing so you must prepare for the greatest day of your life."

The virtual panorama played out in Billy's mind. The kaleidoscope of memories reaching finality. Her transcendence almost complete.

The moment neared… her destiny now forever entwined with Georgy's. He'll help her with the heir she needed as the Supreme One… after he'd provided the sacrifice necessary for her inauguration ceremony.

Billy pounded on, each of her thrusts bring both her and Autumn to the finality of climax. Billy felt her climax reaching its crescendo.

She glanced down at the beautiful female form before her. The light danced across her glistening body. The smoke seemed to twirl in her wild ginger mane.

The moment of mutual climax overwhelmed them both at the same instant Billy brought down her right hand. The flashing blade arced downward into Autumn's sacrificial chest. The moment of life and death… the climax heralded the arrival of the Dead Pussy Society's new Supreme One.

The Diamonds of Myth

"No... that's a load of rotten donkey droppings!" Geel Gert exclaimed. *"Where in the world did you hear such a pile of tripe?"*

His high-pitched voice was by now so strained that it almost crackled. He stared at his companion in utter disbelief.

"Ag man... you've got to believe me. I was in the Red Lion in Upington when I heard the story. The regulars were passing around some peach brandy, you know that wit-blitz from Kanonkop, the stuff everyone is always trying to get their hands on."

Willie was speaking in hushed tones. He was also speaking slowly because Geel Gert wasn't the quickest on the uptake. Rather slow, actually.

"They thought I'd passed out on the juice they were sharing round."

At that point Zach had to strain his ears even more. If he dared move any closer, they may suspect they were being overheard... snooped on. That could be dangerous. The men obviously chose the library because they were looking for a quiet, cool place where they could discuss their plans, away from prying eyes and village gossips.

They'd strolled into the library a few minutes earlier, looking this way and that. Up and down the rows of bookshelves... scouting out the place. They found the partially secluded reading area at the rear of the room.

Something they didn't notice was one of the floor to ceiling shelves being slightly askew. They also didn't realise that behind those racks was a small office, used by the staff for their admin work.
Also unbeknown to them, behind the façade of books was the presence of a youngster. This was Zach's haven... his vanishing hole when the town bullies were after him.

That is how Zach came to know of the story while minding his business... not intentionally eavesdropping.

"OK," said Geel, *"tell me again."*

He waited a few seconds before again urging, *"Come on Willie... you can't want me to believe a story like that. Diamonds enough to buy half the Transvaal? Never!"*

Again his voice was reaching crackling levels.

"Shush man," gasped Willem, *"You're making more noise than a herd of charging buffalo's... you'll soon have the whole town investigating what the commotion is about."*

He rolled his eyes in mock horror. This sidekick of his, what had he done wrong in a previous life to deserve such an oaf as an aid?

"Can't you see the signs all over the place..." he paused and pointed around, *"sorry man, I forgot you can't read. OK... the signs say we must shut-up, so... shut-up before we're kicked out of the place!"*

By now Willem's tone was a bit of a snarl. He was the brain, Geel needed to be reminded of the fact.

"The lot in the Red Lion were saying there are more diamonds at the bottom of the falls than De Beers have in their vaults."

Willem paused for the significance of the statement to sink in.

"The little beauties have been washed down the river for all time... only to be trapped at the bottom of the falls..."

"Ag no man... what's that going to do for two blokes like us?" Geel's question seemed a very valid one... how in fact, would they benefit with this information?

"Easy... one of the fellows in the Red Lion gave me an idea." Willem paused, again, to ensure the dim-witted Geel kept up with him.

"He was drinking his wit-blitz and orange juice through a straw... said it had more kick that way."

"So? What's that got to do with diamonds?" His tone inched upward again.

"Simple stupid... we get a big vacuum cleaner and suck the diamonds out of the hole... that's what we do!" Willem concluded triumphantly.

"No boet, now I know you're touched... all that wit-blitz and sun has got to you." He sighed, even his slow brain told him this was a bit too good to be true.

"Where will you even get a vacuum cleaner to work in the water? All the one's I've ever seen can hardly pick up a paperclip off the floor... now you want me to believe you want us to suck diamonds out of the holes at the bottom of the Augrabies..." his voice trailed off in utter disbelief.

"Listen to me... in the dry season there is almost no water in the holes," another pause, *"when I was in the army we had big pumps... like vacuums, to pump water out of the drains and out of the river... you know, they can work."*

"Ah no man..." Geel was tiring of this tale, *"you can't be serious man..."*

He wanted to get out of the library, he was getting more and more thirsty by the minute. All this thinking was drying out his brain, so he did the best he could... under the circumstances.

"Haven't you heard of the rain god of the locals, they say she protects the diamonds..." this was deep thinking for Geel but he had to put a stop to Willem's mad plan. He didn't want some strange river being sucking him into a hole at the bottom of the waterfall.

"What? Now you're talking piles of bull..." it was Willem's turn to gasp in exasperation, *"big humps of elephant bull!"*

Zach remembered the conversation going this way and that. It turned into more than a conversation, it turned into a debate. It didn't take too long for Willie to get the persuasive upper hand. He coaxed Geel Gert into agreeing that they'd give it at least one shot.

They'd wait for the dry season... then put their plan in action under cover of darkness. They'd sneak into the park with one of the fancy pumps on the back of Willem's pick-up. They'd get away before dawn... rich men, they'd be.

Minutes after the debate subsided the two men left the library. Zach soon forgot the whole episode. However, months later a five-line snippet, almost lost on page seven of the weekly Upington's Kalahari Tribune, caught his attention.

Apparently, the mangled remains of two men were found about five miles below the falls. The paper named the men as a certain Willem Delport and his friend Gert Geel. Strangely, said the article, a very rare, totally unseasonal flash flood passed through the area. The piece further stated that the last time this rare phenomenon occurred was about the time of the First World War, when a group of renegade soldiers attempted to remove diamonds from the pools beneath the falls.

Zach shook his head in disbelief. Yes, it seemed the river god had got the better of the men's greed. Seems she didn't take kindly to thieves wanting to remove her gems.

The Lucky Ones

Martain sat at the table furthest from the solitary light in the dingy room. He breathed in the heavy air laced with stale, swirling peat fumes. The rumpled, multi-coloured rag posing as a tablecloth stained beyond redemption. Beyond redemption? The random thought sparked by the sight of the manky piece of cloth startled Martain. Whose redemption? The word only recently become part of his vocabulary.

Redemption?

Until five weeks' previously the word never played any part in his thought processes. A word that may once have been a meaningless by-product of a faith he'd long turned his back on.

Then, the slim package arrived at the office. The office manager called to say a courier had made advanced contact enquiring after a certain Mr Martain Constantine O'Donnell. The girl asked if it was possible for him to accept the package in person as the courier refused to hand it over without proof of identity.

Martain recalled his surprise. Nobody in South Africa knew the existence of his full names so whoever was sending him something could only be from his very early childhood. He recalled the shiver down his spine and the involuntarily cringing. He recalled shaking like a five Euro note in the sweaty hands of a desperate drunk when he signed the courier's despatch note.

How had his past caught up with him? Who on this planet would have the gall to send a hand couriered package to the leafy Cape Town suburbs? No, who on this planet knew his past so intimately that they addressed the package to Martain Constantine O'Donnell?

The fishmoth scurrying across the table jerked his thoughts back to the present reality. Here he sat, waiting for heaven knows what? He was ravenous. It was hours since the driver had collected him at Dublin International Airport where he'd last had a quick cup of tepid machine coffee. He didn't really want to ask if he could see a menu for fear of offending someone.

He looked around; the dingy, dated decor must have been high fashion when Noah boarded the Ark. The place seemed as if it would rate highly on the environmental hazards listings. He expected to see the health services walk in at any second to close the place down.

His first attempt at flicking the fishmoth off the table failed so he gave it another go. The distraction served to draw his mind away from all the unanswered questions milling in his tired mind. It also served as a perfect cover for the arrival of the slender creature who floated in.

"Ye must be mighty famished?"

The soft, almost lyrical question startled Martain. He looked up to see a pair of smouldering, dark eyes looking down at him. The voice… the eyes? Was she real? Her dark locks tumbled all over the place, framing her pale, delicate features perfectly.

"Hungry?"

The single word floated on the heavy air. Mystery captured in one word. He wondered about the sweet sound. A charm beckoned when she opened her mouth. One sentence, one word? Could this witch be spinning some kind of magic over him?

"Surely lost yer tongue, never ye mind, I shall feed ye."

She disappeared as silently as she'd arrived. Martain wondered about it all. Here he was after almost 30 hour's travel, sitting in a totally foreign environment, being bewitched by a presence who spoke with the voice of an angel. An angel disguised as a witch or a witch masquerading as an angel?

His mind drifted. Thoughts of a distant past crept from the shady recesses of grey. Did he really recognise the green, rolling countryside he'd seen on the way here or was his imagination playing bizarre games?

A faint cord vibrated gently within his core. That voice. Could there be a link with the distant past? Could he know that voice? No, surely not. He absentmindedly scratched his left cheek with his right forefinger, a habit that only ever surfaced when he became distressed or agitated.

"Food, stranger... and a pour of the black stuff?"

Once again the voice caught him totally unawares. He'd been so far away in thought that he'd again missed her appearance. Was she for real? Surely, she must be because she was carrying in his meal.

The nymph bent down to light the candle. Martain caught a brief close-up glimpse of her eyes. His heart skipped a beat, no, about five beats. The breath seemed to rip out of him. He was looking into his own eyes! How?

"Who… who are you?"

His pained words wrenched at his strained vocal cords. She noticed his beseeching eyes.

"Aha, you find your tongue stranger. Eat, you need your strength. Eat and drink, all will be revealed in good time."

Martain gasped, simultaneously bewildered and enchanted. His senses reeled. His confusion and confoundment deepened. Never in all his life had he experienced these strangely convoluted emotions. His mind spun, thoughts gyrated… falling into the distorted abyss of uncontrolled uncertainty.

How could this happen to him? Why was this happening to him? Who was she? Why was he here? Who would be plotting for his senses to be so disrupted? Was the woman a witch or merely an evil spirit?

He felt weak. Could he even dare eat or drink anything in this place? He needed air… space, open space and sunshine but he couldn't summon the energy to run. Those eyes… her graceful elegance. Why did he know the face? A face of an angel stared at him yet he was certain she was a witch. Angel witch… heavenly banshee…deliriously enchanting being.

He took a sip without even realising he was doing so. He took another, then another. The liquid black velvet soothed his raw throat, spreading its cool warmth as it seeped into his tired being. Only in Ireland could you savour such pleasure, that's what the legend said about the stout. He drained the glass.

"Man, that was good…"

His mutter was barely out when she appeared again. She placed another glass on the table.

"Eat now stranger, you cannot be throwing them down without a feed in yer belly."

She removed the empty class and disappeared into the gloom. Martain heeded her advice. He took a small mouthful, unsure if the food would be as good as the beer. He wasn't disappointed. The stew was superb. Stew and stout, as only the Irish can make. It tasted like a homecoming meal but he wasn't sure why.

The more he thought about it the more he realised that even the food and drink added to his confusion. Homecoming meals in a foreign land, how was that possible?

"Those eyes…"

"Those eyes…"

He realised he was muttering the words between mouthfuls.

"Those eyes… they've touched my soul…"

Martain scraped the last tasty morsels from the bowl before gently replacing the fork. He sighed a tired, full bellied, contented sigh as the candle spluttered itself into a smoky demise. Martain leaned back in the chair. He allowed himself to relax just a little or could it be the peat fumes causing his drowsiness? It mattered little because his turmoil lessened as his contentment grew.

Her words echoed in his mind… *eat and drink, all will be revealed in time.* When will that time arrive, he wondered?

"Come, I'll show you to your room for the night or would you enjoy a coffee or whiskey first?"

Martain realised he must have dozed for he didn't have a clue how long she'd been standing there. The room seemed even gloomier so he imagined night had fallen. He was weary but the idea of a strong coffee and an even stronger whiskey sounded too tempting to refuse.

He looked up at the woman. She beckoned for him to move closer to the fire. He did and was pleasantly surprised at the comfort of the old leather recliner. He'd expected a spring or two to jab him in the backside but that didn't happen.

He looked at the fire; the flames were licking at the fresh peat. Yes, he must've been fast asleep for he hadn't seen her adding peat to the fire or lighting the lamps on the mantelpiece.

He loved staring into fires. The flames were mesmerising. They captivated his imagination, often stirring mythical figures from the dark recesses of his mind.

"Coffee or a dram?"

Her soft words drew him back to the moment.

"Would it be rude if I asked for both? A strong black coffee and a glass of good whiskey would go down just fine, if I may?"

He watched her turn to leave.

"Before you go…"

"Yes?"

"Please, you may think I'm extremely rude but please may I ask your name?"

She didn't answer immediately, as if she may have contemplated ignoring his question.

"No, on both counts, you're not rude at all. By all means you may have coffee and whiskey. Alina, that's what they named me… however the odd people around here calls me May. I don't know why…"

"Thank you Alina, thank you for your generosity and kindness. I'm still confused by exactly what's going on but you must please let me know the rates so I can settle the bill."

"All in good time, don't you be worrying about money matters now. Have you ever enjoyed a good Irish?"

"Never in Ireland so I'm looking forward to my first sip, that's a promise."

"Grand, I'll be getting you a drop of the best, locally distilled by the monks at the abbey. Abbey Divine, it's called. You'll only find it here."

Martain relaxed. He recalled his initial surprise when he'd first opened the courier package. That seemed so long ago, even though not much more than a month had passed since he'd read the note.

The words were simple yet somehow he knew he'd have to accept their challenge.

> *'We request you to travel to Ireland on a journey of redemption. All the arrangements have been finalised and included in the package you will find an itinerary as well as the necessary return tickets for the journey.*
> *You will be collected at Dublin International and taken to a place where you will meet your guide. Please ensure that you bring a full set of comfortable wet-weather hiking gear and sturdy boots.'*

That was it. No further details, apart from the itinerary and plane tickets.

A journey of redemption? That was the hook. He'd taken the bait and now here he sat. Alina's reappearance stopped his rearward glance in time. She must be his guide.

"Alina, why am I here? Where will you be taking me?"

"Mind if I join?"

"How could I mind? Is this not your place?"

"No, I'm only here to see to your immediate needs before we head off tomorrow morning."

Alina placed a tray containing their coffee and whiskey on the small coffee table before taking her seat in the other recliner. Even the simple act of sitting down seemed sensual. Martain focused on the delicate lines of her legs. Finely sculpted, he thought.

"You're letting yer thoughts wander too far... again."

Man alive, was she for real, he wondered? Mind reader, mind warper? He was about to make a lame comment about '*just observing what was unfolding*' but though better of it. She'd see through that as well.

"I'll wake ye at three thirty. We must be away here around four. We have a few hours walk ahead of us and we must do it in the dark."

"Why? Is that not a little difficult for someone who doesn't know where they going?"

"We don't need the prying eyes wondering what we're doing. We need to get to a secluded safe house so the best is to go quietly in the dark. Enough said."

Martain heeded her caution. Silence, whiskey and introspection went well together. He decided to rest his scrambled thoughts, as best he could. Tomorrow things may become clearer so it didn't help him to fret now.

"I'll wake you at three thirty. A mug of coffee and a few slices of toast do you? We'll have a full Irish once we reach our destination."

"Make that strong black again please. Toast with a bit of butter will do just great. That should get me into walking mood."

"You did bring your hiking equipment?"

"Yes, all well-worn in and comfortable. The boots have been up and down Table Mountain quite a few times."

"Once you've completed your ablutions and readied yourself please stow all your other belongings in your case. Mind you, you'd want to take a change of comfortable dry clothes with you, the rest you won't be needed to carry along. Your case will be collected so ensure you have everything packed. We do not want to leave clues."

"You have it all worked out, don't you?"

"Fail to plan... plan to fail..."

The old adage sounded more like mockery than mirth but the smile on her face lightened the moment.

"Unless I'm mistaken you should think of finishing that whiskey soon. Can't have you stumbling around in the dark."

"You're a hard task master… I was just beginning to enjoy the brew."

"A little sacrifice is required now. The rewards will be great."

Martain wondered why he thought he had to believe every word this woman uttered. He wasn't yet fully comfortable in her presence, even though he'd relaxed considerably.

"Drink up, I'll show you your room. You will be comfortable, that I assure you."

Martain followed obediently. He could do with sleep so he didn't object at being summoned to bed well before nine. Sleep came easily and quickly. He didn't have a bother in the world until Alina woke him the next morning. The hike wouldn't be too pleasant, seemingly the rainfall had intensified during the night.

"Come, time to get a move on, have your coffee and toast, we must leave soon. Could I have your spare clothes? I'll look after them on the way up."

Ten minutes later they stepped out of the warm cottage into the pouring rain.

"Keep as close behind me as possible. We cannot use flashlight yet so the going will be tricky. Make sure you step firmly, the path is rocky so we shouldn't be slipping much in the mud, if we don't step off the path."

Fifty-five minutes later Alina paused beneath an overhang.

"Catch your breath, we need our full wits about us for the assent. The first light of dawn will soon be penetrating the gloom."

She pointed at what must be the slope ahead. Martain peered through the falling rain but try as hard as he could he didn't see any sigh of a slope.

"We'll have to get up the first part of the slope as soon as possible. We can't chance anyone spotting us from below."

He wondered if he should venture a thought. Surely, if they couldn't see three meters in front of them no one would see them from below. He didn't have to ask; it was as if she was mindreading again.

"We can never be too safe, we could have a break in the rain and be caught out in the open with flash lights, better we make it to the secluded part of the walk where we can reassess."

Witchery or telepathy? It freaked him that Alina was seemingly thinking and reacting for him. Yet, although he was perturbed, he was also enchanted by her voice. The lilting melody drew him onward, like the Pied Pipers flute. He plodded on, trying to focus on where she was placing her feet. On another day he may have admired the scenery or even the fine form leading him onward but on this day it was all about one foot in front of the other.

Martain lost track of time. He didn't even notice that daylight was trying it hardest to dispel some of the rain's gloom. The murky wet, swirling breeze up here on the mountainside intensified their sodden misery. He had no clue how Alina could have a clue where they were or if they were even going in the right direction. He was wet to the core and cold to the bone.

He was so intent on following her that he stumbled into her when she stopped. He managed a feeble apology even as she held out her hand to help him steady himself.

"Not what you'd call a leisurely Sunday stroll.

"No, more… like an… infantry… route march… to hell."

He gasped the words.

"We can relax now; we've reached the Forgotten Valley. The walk is almost level and the light better. Life will be easy now."

"Wet, cold and easy."

"You can't have it all your own way… soon you'll be warm and have a belly full of fry. I take it you'll break your healthy dietary rules for a Full Irish."

"Must you joke about food now? I could eat a small horse. A full fry it will be… everything but the beans, please."

"Fussy too… doesn't only speak funny but is fussy as well."

The rain eased sufficiently for Martain to get an idea of the countryside they were walking through. This, he thought, must be why they describe the west of Ireland as wild. It looked deserted and lonely, not a place for living a comfortable existence.

They entered dense woodland which restricted the view of the countryside. Thirty minutes later they broke out of the constraints of the thicket into a large clearing where they set eyes on the first signs of human habitation seen since leaving the cottage hours before.

A walled enclosure appeared out of the rainy gloom. Martain could make out roofs of building and a steeple beyond. Alina led him onward, until they reached a small wooden door almost completely obscured by ivy. You'd only find the door if you knew it existed.

Alina felt in the vegetation around the stone frame until she found the bell pull. She tugged at the rope in a set pattern.

"We'll be inside within minutes. Nothing a warm shower and dry clothes won't fix."

Within minutes they were following a figure in a monk's habit. Martain wasn't introduced. No words were spoken. There'd been feint tapping on the inside of the door and when Alina replied with more coded knocks the door was opened by their mysterious host. Alina leaned closer to whisper,

"Sorry, I forgot to mention, don't speak to anyone, try not to make eye contact either."

The subservient following is becoming a way of life now thought Martain.

They were let into a door of a cottage at the far end of the compound.

"You'll find an on-suite in your room, I'll have your clothes on your bed by the time you step out of the shower."

Alina opened a door and pointed in.

"There you go..."

Martain stepped in and headed straight for the on-suite. He turned on the shower to get it up to temperature while he stripped out of his clothes. They were in varying states of wetness. He must have been carrying about ten kilograms of water along with him for most of the way. The puddle on the floor increased in size as he dropped item after item on the pile of sodden cloth.

Ten minutes later he stepped out of the shower and towelled himself dry. He found his clothes where Alina had left them. When he stepped out of the room to find Alina he felt like a new man.

"Nothing like a good brisk morning walk to get the appetite going."

"You men are all the same, your bellies and your carnal needs, that's all you ever seem to think of."

"Well, you did promise a Full Irish if I made it here in one piece, didn't you?"

"Come, sit... your reward will soon be forthcoming."

He followed her advice and sat himself down at the end of a well-worn table. The pale wood bleached by many years of scrubbing. Everything in the kitchen seemed to have been scrubbed for a very long time. Functional and clean, very clean. In fact, he wondered if there were many operating theatres that were scrubbed so thoroughly.

"I'd better not mess or spill… seems there will be someone to dish out lashes if I do."

"It's not that bad. What you see is just a product of years of pious devotion… and possibly boredom. Let's eat, I can do with a bit of sustenance."

Again Martain obeyed. He was finding it easy to just do as he was told, for fear of stirring her wrath. He still suspected that she'd place him under a spell if he gave her any reason to do so.

Martain looked up as the door opened to see a man dressed in a habit enter.

"Meet Peter, he's here to share some information with us."

"Hello Alina, hello Martain. Welcome to our refuge, welcome to the Constantine Abbey."

Martain felt the hairs on the back of his neck stand on end, the accompanying cold shiver down his back warned him to be on the alert. The name of the abbey… surely not coincidental?

"The look in your eye tells me something is amiss."

Martain remained silent for a few moments. His gaze alternated between Alina and Peter, trying to fathom any signs of foreboding.

"No, maybe not amiss, just too strange to be true. I'm beginning to wonder what I've let myself in for."

"You may well wonder. All is above board, I assure you. Strange but above board."

"Alina is a local but she is very much part of the story. She may or may not have worked out some of the details but for clarity I will begin by taking the story of the abbey's history back about a century."

Peter paused to confirm that he had their undivided attention. They both nodded, so he continued.

"About eighty years ago a young lady arrived at the abbey in a bad way. She was heavily pregnant with nowhere to go. You can imagine, those days it was more than taboo to get in that way out of wedlock. Please give me a second to pour a coffee. Anyone care to join me?"

Martain accepted, Alina declined.

"Yes please, one can never have too much coffee… strong black please."

Peter continued the story as he was sorting out the coffees.

"The abbey folk were at a bit of a loss. Because the place is so secluded not many outsiders even knew of the abbey's existence, so catering for pregnancies up here was unheard of. The Abbot and Mother Superior decided to send the young lady to one of the Order's other parishes but the arrival of the baby put pay to that."

"Not long after the birth of the little girl the decision was made to transfer mother and baby to the monastery in Co Sligo. There, mother and child could be better cared for."

Martain held up his hand. Peter stopped his monologue.

"Why did the pregnant lady come all the way up here if there were easier places to get to?"

"It was rumoured that the girl was a mistress of one of the minor royals who had a summer residence on the shores of Loch Ferly. An old caretaker at the residence knew of the abbey up here and for secrecy purposes they brought the girl here."

"OK, I'll take that as some sort of explanation but it still sounds a little illogical to me. I can't really imagine a heavily pregnant woman trekking all the way we did. Just too difficult."

"Oh, is that what's bothering you. Sorry, I'm being vague. There are two alternate routes to the abbey. Much easier. The young lady was probably dropped at the main gate by carriage."

"Then why the flipping hell did you make me have to do the martyr's path?"

Peter and Alina noted Martain's obvious agitation. Alina was first to speak.

"Do you think I enjoyed that little county wander? We had to bring you in the difficult, secret way. The press watch this place all the time. They're constantly looking for a story... for scandal, for the next sensational scoop."

Martain chose to remain silent. He concentrated on his food, not looking up at the two of them. Why was he being drawn into all of this? He had the distinct impression that he was going to get answers to yet unasked questions that he may not want to hear.

He sipped at the coffee until the mug was empty.

"I'll have a bit more of that... if there's still some going."

Peter took the mug from him and refilled it.

"Looks like I'll have to make another brew. Alina, any for you?"

"No... a bit of tea will do me just fine, thanks."

They remained silent while Peter busied himself with the brews. Each wondered how the following snippets of information would be accepted or interpreted. Peter eventually spoke.

"A few of the abbeys and monasteries here in the west have really unsavoury blotches on their records. A few years ago, two separate investigations uncovered very disturbing discoveries. In one find a pit was uncovered. It contained the skeletal remains of new-born babies as well as those of a few women."

"Wow. On the premises of a monastery?"

"Yes… seems our religious folk didn't act too Godly at times."

All Martain could do was shake his head from side to side. He wondered if his initial curiosity could have lead him into accepting an invitation into a world of intrigue that would have been better avoided.

"I don't really know what to say or think. Why would I be here if I wasn't in some obscure way linked with all of this?"

"You're right, both you and Alina are linked."

"OK… before my mind gets in a total jumble… you began the story with a pregnant lady arriving here about eighty years ago. Then you went onto more recent scandals. How are the two related? They must be… otherwise you wouldn't have told us about it in the first place."

"That girl with the baby is the key to the tale. She went back to the manor house when she'd lost all signs of the pregnancy. The father of the baby, the third son of Lord Ennis, wanted to have the little girl around so he arranged for one of his other staff members to adopt the child. So, he had his mistress and his child around."

"However, it seems it was a bit of like mother like daughter. Apparently, she hardly made it to her eighteenth birthday when she needed to be spirited off to have her first child."

Peter paused. He indicated to their cups.

"More?"

"No thanks, enough caffeine for one day."

"Alina?"

When she shook her head he rose and started clearing away their breakfast crockery. He waved Alina's assistance away.

"No thanks… this is my space, I'll soon be done and then we can get back to the story. Why don't you go through to the sitting room? You'll be more comfortable there."

"Martain waited for Alina to be seated before he spoke."

"What do you make of all this? Have you any idea how we're linked to this tale?"

"I'm a little too scared to venture a guess really. I have a feeling those pregnancies have something to do with us. I have long had suspicions that I was somehow linked to the abbey."

"How, why?"

"I often wondered, as I grew up, why it seemed I got special treatment when I visited here."

"What do you mean… special treatment, by who?"

Alina leaned closer to Martain, not wanting to risk Peter overhearing.

"I would stay here most holidays. There were always two or three nuns who took special care of me. Treats, cookies and biscuit found their way into my diet quite often. Then there was an abbot who visited often. These folk took the role of my family."

"Do you think they could really be your family? Could you have been the child of one of those nuns you speak of? Did you ever…"

Martain cut his question short as Peter appeared in the doorway. He'd have to wait for another time to complete his sentence. Peter made himself comfortable after placing water and soft drinks on the coffee table. He cleared his throat before continuing the story.

"Fine, let's continue. Firstly, let me get back to the uncovering of scandals. I mentioned two separate discoveries in the last few years. When the dust settled down after the discovery of all the skeletons in the disused septic pit the questions began. How was it possible for the religious orders to have hidden such crimes for so long? I haven't got any answers and don't want to start a debate on the subject. I want you to keep the information in the back of your mind for now because I want to discuss the other uncover."

Peter reached for a bottle of water and took a long sip before speaking again. He gestured at the drinks, indicating that they should help themselves. He cleared his throat again.

"Please pardon all my throat clearing, I'm not used to all this talking. It's a little heavy on the throat. Never mind my throat… let's try to get to where I want to head. The other scandal was a little less obvious. It became apparent, as the enquiries continued, that some of the monasteries were supplying babies on demand."

Peter turned to look at their faces for reaction. He saw what he expected. Dumfounded shock. Martain's momentarily open jaw silently mouthing unspoken words. Alina's wide-eyed dismay betrayed a hint of something else. Peter had an inkling that she'd worked out how she was involved.

"I've got a feeling I was born here... am I right?"

"Hold that idea for a moment, if you will. I'll fast forward the history a little. I've got as far Lord Ennis's illegitimate daughter now being in the baby way. That young lady, indecently, was named Alina."

Alina's surprise turned to a smile.

"Nothing you say would surprise me anymore."

"Let's continue… the lord did what he knew best, he arranged for Alina to have her baby here at the abbey. This time he didn't have a problem with Alina returning to the manor house, remember she was for all intents and purposes not his daughter. So, our man had his mistress, his daughter and his granddaughter at the manor house."

"Hold on Peter, the more I think of it the more I'm wondering if I really had to travel all this way to come and learn about all of this. Knowing about some minor noble and his illegitimate family seems a little irrelevant, don't you think? I mean… wouldn't you…"

Martain was about to continue but Peter wasn't going to have any of it.

"Maybe not when I tell you it's your family I'm telling you about."

Peter's sharp retort shut Martain up. It also drew a gasp from Alina.

"What? Am I correct in assuming we're related?"

Alina gestured at Martain and then herself. Within seconds their expressions changed from surprise to realisation. Martain sat in stunned silence. He was quite happy for Alina to do all the talking.

"How? Cousins… distant, near?"

"No, close, siblings in fact. But we'll get to that later… Martain, your impatience has me getting ahead of myself."

Peter paused a few seconds to gather his thoughts and get the chronology of the story flowing again.

"Martain, we had to get you here. What was it the note asked you to do?"

"Come to Ireland… what was the word… mmm, redemption, that's right, come to Ireland on a journey of redemption."

Peter remained silent. He left them with their thoughts for a few minutes. He waited until they were ready to continue.

"Who's redemption?"

"Maybe all of ours… mostly though, someone you'll be meeting later today."

"OK… I have a feeling you need to fill us in on more of the background. So, please excuse me for a minute or two for a rest break before you continue."

When Martain returned the coffee table was laid out with fresh bread, ham, cheese, preserves and what looked like real farm butter. A carafe of red wine complimented the food.

"You eat while I talk on. I have to keep going if we must make our appointment this afternoon."

"This all looks like local produce… apart from the wine, I suspect."

"You're right. The wine we get from a French abbey… in exchange for our whiskey."

Martain noted the hint of pride in Peter's voice. Yes, these folk did things to the best of their ability, that was evident. The tastes and smells alone was sufficient to reinforce Peter's pride.

"Ok Martain. We had to bring you in the hard way, for fear of you getting seen by the locals. Everyone is constantly looking for the next story to flog to the ever-curious media. Nothing like a bit of sensationalism to sell a few more rag sheets."

"Why would I cause any interest? I'm not known here."

"That's the whole point. If you were seen arriving in the village below or being dropped off at any of the pubs or B&B's in the area the questions would immediately begin. Then, heaven forbid, someone connects you to any of the local religious establishments, we'd have the press here within hours. They're hungry for a story. They're all searching for the next pit of skeletons, real or imaginary. You must understand… the old Orders are fair game. Everyone who thinks they have the remotest case wants to make a quick buck."

Martain couldn't contain his frustration any longer.

"So, why did I have to come here in the first place? Why not meet somewhere in Dublin? Why come to Ireland in the first place?"

"Because the person who requested you to come cannot travel. That person is too frail. That's the person you'll be meeting later."

Peter allowed his words to sink in. He wanted Martain and Alina to come to terms with all he had shared before delving further into the finer details of the tale.

"If you want a short break before we continue to chat between yourselves, I'll leave the room for a bit. I have to think of preparing the evening meal so it will be good for me."

Peter didn't wait for confirmation. He was up before either of them had time to think. He wanted them to try and piece the story together. He felt that it would lessen the potential shock he still had to share.

Martain and Alina sat without speaking until the door closed behind Peter.

"You know Alina; I've had a funny feeling about you from the moment I first set eyes on you. That's it… it's your eyes!"

Alina's words didn't really come as a surprise.

"You're my brother, aren't you?"

Her soft whisper cleaved the air, leaving emotional turbulence rebounding off the walls of their souls. Martain rose unsteadily. He wanted to hold this person who he'd only met the day before. He wanted to comfort her but he knew he was craving her comforting.

Martain understood and he sensed Alina's understanding.

"Redemption, our redemption story."

That's how Peter found them when he returned later. Both softly weeping, gently hugging each other. Long lost siblings clinging desperately onto the promise of new beginnings.

"I see you've found each other. There's really little else for me to say."

His words were soft and gentle.

"Yes, little else to add but to fill in a few details before I take you to meet the person who wants you here."

He waited for them to sit before he continues.

"I know it must all be draining to discover what you're finding out. It must be shattering to realise your whole perception of your past may not be what you'd always believed it to be."

"Martain, you were adopted by the O'Donnell's, with one strict reservation. Your names. Martain from the Abbey Constantine. Little did the folk here know that the O'Donnell's would leave the area and settle in South Africa within a year of your adoption. Alina, you were never adopted out. You were simply placed with the Kelly's not long after your birth. It was easily done as Irene Kelly had lost her second child at full term. In your case, the Kelly's were asked to name you Alina."

"Why were the names so important? Why did both of us have to have the names we've lived with all our lives?"

"Your birthparents named you after an obscure twelfth century French saint. Well, some say she was a saint although the official Roman Martyrology doesn't list her name. That's all I'll say on the matter now, I'm not at liberty to say too much."

"What I don't get is our link with the scandals. Why all the secrecy and why should we fear any recrimination?"

"Simply put? You were born to a nun. Your father was a monk. You were pre-order adoption babies. Until reality intervened. But I'm getting ahead of myself again. I think you're about as ready as you'll ever be for the next step of this journey. Come, it's time for me to introduce you the person I mentioned earlier."

Peter rose and gestured for them to follow. Thankfully the rain had stopped so the walk to the next cottage didn't result in another drenching. Peter knocked a few times before cracking open the door slightly.

"Hello… we're here, may we come in?"

They waited for a few seconds before Peter pushed open the door. He was obviously at home here too. He waved them in after him. This cottage was identical to the one they'd just come from so they quickly found their bearings.

"Sit, I'll be back in a moment."

Peter returned a few minutes later. He was supporting a stooped old lady. Her petite frame struggling even with Peter's assistance. Peter helped her into the old leather reclined near the fireplace. Martain and Alina watch on intently. Each looking for the link. They didn't have to wait long. Their simultaneous gasps reverberated through the room at the moment the old lady raised her head.

"Those eyes! Our eyes!"

The old lady's wrinkled face softened as her smile broadened.

"Welcome my children."

The three words galvanised the mood in the room. Martain and Alina visibly perked up, ready for the next revelations of truth. Even Peter, who must have known much of the story, seemed excited.

"Mother?"

Alina's whisper carried the emotions of a generation. Her one word released unknown tensions as if it were the popping of long corked champagne.

"Yes my children, I am your mother. It is I who has asked you to visit me. It is I who wants… no needs, the truth to be known. I cannot go to my grave without seeking redemption."

Martain couldn't get a word out. He sat in stunned silence. Staring at the wrinkled old face with the snow white locks and the lively, smouldering dark eyes. What had those eyes seen in their long life. What stories are locked in that brain? What horrors? What pain or joy? How much time would they need to find all the answers?

The silence lingered. Neither Alina or Martain wanted to be the one to break the mood of expectant anticipation. What if they were disappointed or unfulfilled by what they were going to hear?

Peter sensed their hesitance and broke the silence for them.

You wondered about the relevance of your names. I'm sure Mary will explain…"

"You know you were named after a French saint, don't you? Yes. Saint Alina Martain's feast day was 20 October… yes, as you well know, your birthday."

She watched their eyes, she watched their reaction. One of acknowledgement. She watched them turn to each other in recognition.

"Yes, my children, you are twins. That, and the fact that you arrived early, had a massive effect on all our lives. You see, we fell in love, your father and me. What began as an inquisitive experiment in lovemaking, yes… ended as love."

Martain's surprise got the better of him.

"Wait one… are you telling me nuns and monks were allowed to have affairs? Are you telling me the Orders allowed that kind of thing to carry on? No, worse still, are you telling me they condoned it? I was always under the impression that the babies born in monasteries were those of women arriving from outside for help and shelter. Am I wrong?"

Peter thought it better to explain, to lessen the burden on Mary.

"Yes and no. In the dark days those babies often ended in the pits. Until someone realised there was a perfectly good market out there for adoption babies. Also, it's a well-known rumour that nuns occasionally fell pregnant even while in the convents and monasteries. I'm afraid the primeval procreation urge will always be with mankind, even when they choose a life of supposed celibacy."

"Mary… mother, tell us a little more about us. Why did you want to meet us if we were supposed to be born for adoption?"

"Alina… my daughter, Martain my son. How sweet to say your names. You were never meant for adoption. As I mentioned earlier, we fell in love so when I did fall pregnant we wanted the Abbot and Mother Superior to think the baby was going for adoption. You see, adopting out babies was fine… however, falling in love was taboo!"

"The Church would never condone two people falling in love under their roof. So, we made a plan. I would run away. It wouldn't be too difficult to go back to the old life at the estate. Remember, oh… maybe you haven't been filled in. I was born here at the abbey but grew up on the estate. I'm the lord's granddaughter."

Martain eventually found his voice.

"This gets more interesting by the minute. I believe you're telling us we're the great grandchildren of some royal."

"Minor royal but yes, you are. However, I left the estate because I felt called to serve here at my birthplace. I wanted to live the life of seclusion and celibacy, but love got in the way."

"Mary, were you one of the nuns who used to spoil me when I was little? Remember, when I visited in the holidays."

"Yes, we had to be very careful, that's why I was always with others when I was near you. The original plan was for Martain to also come up here in the holidays but then the O'Donnell's moved away. We could do absolutely nothing then to see you."

"Mary, my turn, if I may? I often wondered where the money came from to send me to university. I know my parents battled financially but yet they got me through college, even when at times I was certain they didn't have much food on their plates."

"I hope you appreciated what they did for you."

"Yes, they were comfortable in their latter years. It was easy for me to look after their finances… they deserved to have it easier in their retirement."

"You're right… we did contribute as best we could. We didn't have much and remember… those days the exchange rates were far from as favourable as today."

"Your father always managed to stay in contact with your adoptive parents and pass on money. That was his pledge to both of you."

"But hold on, I still don't get it… why the need for the journey now? What prompted you? Why arrange for me to come over from South Africa at this point in time?"

"We'd spoken, for quite some time, to get you together but there always seemed something in the way. The invitation note you received was typed and sent the day before your father passed away. He made me promise I'd do it, for both our sakes."

"Oh no! How awful for you. Here we are questioning you while we haven't even found out about you and your loss. Your grief must still be immense."

"No, ask away. I'm prepared for your lifetime of questions. Almost as prepared as I was for your father's passing… he was so very ill toward the end… we all knew the inevitable was on the way. Our only regret wasn't seeing you together before he passed on. Fortunately, we were spared your loss at birth so we lived our lives in hope of seeing you together."

"But you did suffer our loss not long after our birth, didn't you?"

"Giving you away was immeasurably difficult at that time but it was vastly more acceptable than what may have happened if our superiors had discovered twins. It all worked out as Divine destiny had planned it. I didn't have to run away from the abbey. The two of you put pay to that. Firstly, you surprised us by being twins and then you arrived early, before I could get down the mountain."

"So, what did you do?"

Mary was showing signs of fatigue but kept going. Peter interrupted.

"Mary, we have long days to talk about the past. Now you must rest."

"No… I'm fine, for now. We should get the truth out now, while the questions are fresh. I don't want Alina and Martain sleeping another night not knowing."

She paused for a minute or so, catching her breath and gathering her thoughts before she continued.

"Where were we? Oh, yes… what did we do? Simple really… we hid you for the first weeks of your lives. You may have arrived early but you were healthy and you soon put on weight. Your father arranged your adoption before the superiors got the wiser. Then, just as easily, he smuggled you out one by one and delivered you to new parents."

"So…what happened when the superiors began asking where your baby was? Surely you had to produce at least one child?"

"Well, as you say… we had to produce one child and that was very easily arranged. Remember, Irene Kelly lost her baby at full term. The timing was perfect… you were the lucky ones… your premature arrival saved you from the bone pit!"

The End

Be on the lookout – soon – for the next collection in the series… tentatively called…

True Stories and Other Lies

Thank you and good night!

aj.vosse@gmail.com

Printed in Great Britain
by Amazon

27838281R00077